WELCOME TO NEW ORLEANS...

...where Voodoo Night brings tourists and natives alike to Chez Camille, a popular French Quarter restaurant. But this week there's more than crawfish being served. Murder is on the menu!

...where the descendants of famed priestess Marie Laveaux assemble at the mausoleum in the dead of night and ghostly fingers of fog rise from the murky ground...

...where the stately mansions of the rich hide scandal and secrets in the luxurious Garden District...

...and where three long-lost cop brothers must unite to find a killer before he sends an unlucky charm to his next victim. The same blood runs through their veins, but Jordan, Liam and Zach are as different as night and day. Still, when they put on the uniform of the NOPD, there's nothing but justice on their minds. Justice and—when the sun goes down on the Crescent City—love....

Dear Harlequin Intrigue Reader,

The holidays are upon us! We have six dazzling stories of intrigue that will make terrific stocking stuffers—not to mention a well-deserved reward for getting all your shopping done early....

Take a breather from the party planning and unwrap Rita Herron's latest offering, *A Warrior's Mission*—the next exciting installment of COLORADO CONFIDENTIAL, featuring a hot-blooded Cheyenne secret agent! Also this month, watch for *The Third Twin*—the conclusion of Dani Sinclair's HEARTSKEEP trilogy that features an identical triplet heiress marked for murder who seeks refuge in the arms of a rugged lawman.

The joyride continues with *Under Surveillance* by highly acclaimed author Gayle Wilson. This second book in the PHOENIX BROTHERHOOD series has an undercover agent discovering that his simple surveillance job of a beautiful woman-in-jeopardy is filled with complications. Be there from the start when B.J. Daniels launches her brand-new miniseries, CASCADES CONCEALED, about a close-knit northwest community that's visited by evil. Don't miss the first unforgettable title, *Mountain Sheriff*.

As a special gift-wrapped treat, three terrific stories in one volume. Look for *Boys in Blue* by reader favorites Rebecca York, Ann Voss Peterson and Patricia Rosemoor about three long-lost New Orleans cop brothers who unite to reel in a killer. And rounding off a month of nonstop thrills and chills, a pregnant woman and her wrongly incarcerated husband must set aside their stormy past to bring the real culprit to justice in *For the Sake of Their Baby* by Alice Sharpe.

Best wishes to all of our loyal readers for a joyous holiday season!

Enjoy,

Denise O'Sullivan
Senior Editor
Harlequin Intrigue

BOYS IN BLUE

REBECCA YORK
RUTH GLICK WRITING AS REBECCA YORK

ANN VOSS PETERSON

PATRICIA ROSEMOOR

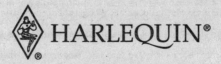

HARLEQUIN®

TORONTO • NEW YORK • LONDON
AMSTERDAM • PARIS • SYDNEY • HAMBURG
STOCKHOLM • ATHENS • TOKYO • MILAN • MADRID
PRAGUE • WARSAW • BUDAPEST • AUCKLAND

ISBN 0-373-22745-0

BOYS IN BLUE

Copyright © 2003 by Harlequin Books S.A.

The publisher acknowledges the copyright holders of the individual works as follows:

JORDAN
Copyright © 2003 by Ruth Glick

LIAM
Copyright © 2003 by Ann Voss Peterson

ZACHARY
Copyright © 2003 by Patricia Pinianski

This edition published by arrangement with Harlequin Books S.A.

® and TM are trademarks of the publisher. Trademarks indicated with ® are registered in the United States Patent and Trademark Office, the Canadian Trade Marks Office and in other countries.

Visit us at www.eHarlequin.com

Printed in U.S.A.

ABOUT THE AUTHORS

Award-winning, bestselling novelist **Ruth Glick, who writes as Rebecca York,** is the author of close to eighty books, including her popular 43 LIGHT STREET series for Harlequin Intrigue. Ruth says she has the best job in the world. Not only does she get paid for telling stories, she's also the author of twelve cookbooks. Ruth and her husband, Norman, travel frequently, researching locales for her novels and searching out new dishes for her cookbooks.

Ever since she was a little girl making her own books out of construction paper, **Ann Voss Peterson** wanted to write. So when it came time to choose a major at the University of Wisconsin, creative writing was the only choice. Of course, writing wasn't a *practical* choice—one needs to earn a living. So Ann found jobs ranging from proofreading legal transcripts to working with quarter horses to washing windows. But no matter how she earned her paycheck, she continued to write the type of stories that captured her heart and imagination— romantic suspense. Ann lives near Madison, Wisconsin, with her husband, her two young sons, her Border collie and her quarter horse mare. Ann loves to hear from readers. E-mail her at ann@annvosspeterson.com or visit her Web site at annvosspeterson.com.

To research her novels, **Patricia Rosemoor** is willing to swim with dolphins, round up mustangs or howl with wolves—"whatever it takes to write a credible tale." She's the author of contemporary, historical and paranormal romances, but her first love has always been romantic suspense. She won both a *Romantic Times* Career Achievement Award in Series Romantic Suspense and a Reviewer's Choice Award for one of her more than thirty Intrigue novels. She's now writing erotic thrillers for Harlequin Blaze. Ms. Rosemoor would love to know what you think of this story. Write to Patricia Rosemoor at P.O. Box 578297, Chicago, IL 60657-8297 or via e-mail at Patricia@PatriciaRosemoor.com, and visit her Web site at http://PatriciaRosemoor.com.

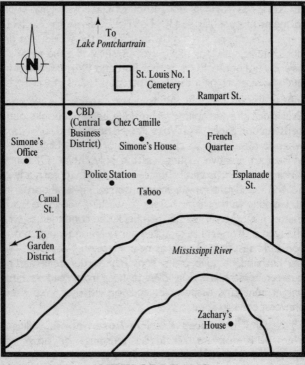

NEW ORLEANS

SUSPECT LINEUP

Odette LaFantary—Did her dark eyes conceal a voodoo queen, a charlatan…or a killer?

Sadie Marceau—This sweet old lady hid more than her share of secrets in her diary….

Helen Gaylord—Did this spinster cherish her sister Sadie…or resent her?

Marie Germain—No one knew much about Odette's tight-lipped new assistant.

Spiro DeLyon—His last meal was a killer….

Miss Lulu DeLyon—Grieving widow…or conniving fortune hunter?

Lisa Cantro—She begged Odette for a spell to bring her good luck…but did it?

Tony Fortune—The slight man cast a big shadow….

Gary Yancy—The fancy-dressing detective had his own brand of justice for the Crescent City….

JORDAN

REBECCA YORK

RUTH GLICK WRITING AS REBECCA YORK

Chapter One

Camille DuPree peered anxiously through the lace-curtained front window of her restaurant, Chez Camille. The man who had been loitering on the other side of Burgundy Street for the past twenty minutes was still there—standing in the shadows where she couldn't see him clearly.

Was he the mugger who had assaulted one of her patrons? Or was he from the security company she'd hired to make sure nobody else ended up getting hit over the head and robbed after enjoying her crawfish étouffée?

Realizing her hands were clenched into fists at her sides, she made an effort to relax. There was no point letting the customers she had left see her anxiety.

Until the mugging incident two weeks ago, Chez Camille had been on the fast track to culinary success. Her sweet-potato pie and Cajun bisque had been the New Orleans dishes of the season.

Now people were talking about her for the wrong reasons. And she was paying for ads in the newspaper assuring her customers of their safety.

A flurry of movement at the door made her heart

accelerate. But it was only Sadie Marceau and her sister, Helen Gaylord, bustling through the front door.

She gave the portly, older women a warm smile. "Good to see you."

"We wouldn't miss Voodoo Night for the world," Helen answered as she got out her purse and handed over the evening's fifty-dollar admission price. "Oh, I love that black-beaded dress. It's perfect for you. Nineteen twenties, right?"

"Yes. I got it at Glad Rags."

"Janet would have loved it," Helen murmured, referring to Janet Phillippe, a woman in her eighties who, until her death a month ago, had been a regular at the Thursday-night ceremonies.

Camille talked for a moment with the sisters about how much they all missed the senior member of the group, then Sadie asked, "What goodies are you feeding us tonight?"

"I've got a wonderful shrimp remoulade, some of those stuffed oysters you love and a pecan torte," Camille answered.

Sadie made a beeline for the food table, while Helen went to greet friends.

Camille glanced at the various people seated at her tile-topped tables. Most of them were middle-aged and upper-middle class and enthralled by the idea of flirting with the dark and dangerous.

A month ago, Camille had been thinking it might be time to cancel these Thursday-night ceremonies. Now she was thankful for the business they brought in.

Spiro DeLyon and his much younger wife, Miss Lulu, had come early for dinner, as had their friend Tony Fortune. She didn't much like Tony, but she kept that opinion to herself. He was sitting next to a couple of tourists from Philadelphia who had also dined at the restaurant.

At the next table was Lisa Cantro, who'd told the others she'd lost her home in a hurricane a year ago and also recently lost her job. She was hoping that voodoo would reverse her fortunes and was listening wide-eyed to a tale about a man who had asked the priestess for a protective voodoo charm. In a subsequent rainstorm, all the houses in the neighborhood were flooded but his.

Camille had heard that story before. And other testimonials. Privately she was thinking that if voodoo worked, the police would have already caught the mugger who was playing hell with her own fortunes, since the first ceremony after the incident had featured a plea to the *loa*, the voodoo pantheon of gods, to bring the perp to justice. As far as she could see, it hadn't worked.

Her thoughts were interrupted by a tall young man. "Is, uh, this the place where, uh, they're having the voodoo ceremony?" he asked, his voice barely above a whisper.

"Yes."

The willowy brunette with him giggled.

"The cover charge is fifty dollars a person, which includes our refreshment buffet," Camille said, gesturing toward the table at the side of the room.

He didn't blink at the price, and she collected a hundred dollars in cash. Turning back to the door, she tensed as she spotted the man from across the street coming toward her. When she saw he was wearing the uniform of Garland Security, she started to relax. Then she saw his face, and the breath froze in her lungs.

It couldn't be.

Even as she told herself she was seeing things, she

knew it was Jordan O'Reilly. He was as tall as she remembered—just over six feet. With the same dark hair and dark brows. And he was just as heart-breakingly handsome.

He pulled the door open, and they stood facing each other for the first time in six years.

Momentarily disoriented, she clamped her fingers over the edge of the nearest table. His familiar features were harder, more cynical. And she suspected the lines at the corners of his eyes weren't from laughter.

"Wh-what are you doing here?" she stammered, overcome by the emotions swirling through her. "I thought you were with the police force."

JORDAN WAITED a beat before answering, fighting the sudden breathless feeling that gripped his chest. He hadn't been lurking on the other side of the street by accident. No, he'd been putting off the moment he was going to have to face Camille DuPree.

Clearing his throat, he answered, "Yes, I'm with the New Orleans Police Department. But I'm earning some extra income. You have any objections to that?"

He knew he sounded as if he was issuing a challenge, but he couldn't make his voice any less strident.

"Of course not," she murmured.

Up close he could see she was as slim and lovely and unreachable as he remembered. Only now she was all grown up with her blond hair in an upsweep and her high cheekbones accented with a bit of blusher. Out on her own, without her precious family fluttering around. Her father had died ten years ago, but her mom was still in charge of the family mansion. And she had a whole slew of rich snobby aunts and uncles and cousins who were always in and out of the house.

But they weren't here now. And she was in trouble. That was the reason he was here.

The morning he'd seen the article in the newspaper about the mugging, he'd felt something inside his chest turn over. Even after everything that had happened, he'd wanted to come charging to her rescue. So when the job had appeared in the Garland Security computer, he'd asked for it.

Was she as uptight about this meeting as he was? he wondered, then realized she was speaking again.

"Come in. Can I offer you something to eat?" she said, her upper-class gracious-hostess personality firmly in place.

"Not while I'm on duty," he answered, then went still as he spotted Spiro DeLyon. Apparently the man and his pretty redheaded wife had arrived before Jordan had come on shift.

He cursed under his breath. He'd arrested DeLyon for DWI a few months ago. Too bad the man had so much clout in the city—it was probably the reason Jordan hadn't gotten the promotion he'd been expecting.

Their eyes locked, and the businessman's jaw firmed.

Jordan looked away first. An ornate bronze dagger studded with jewels was lying on a nearby table, along with some other voodoo paraphernalia. Probably because he was nervous, Jordan picked up the knife and turned it over in his hands. He put it down abruptly as a bead curtain at the back of the room opened and a tall, light-skinned African-American woman stepped out, regal in her simple white gown and white head cloth. Odette LaFantary.

He'd heard about her, of course. Everybody had. She owned a shop called Taboo that sold natural cosmetics and voodoo paraphernalia. A strange combination, but it seemed to be working for her.

She was followed into the room by six assistants. The two men wore only short vests and loincloths, and carried primitive-looking drums. The four women were dressed in shifts made of bright Kente cloth and carried bells.

After fanning out in a circle near the back wall, the men sat down on the polished wooden floor and began to play an insistent rhythm on the drums. The women stayed on their feet, dancing and shaking their bells in time to the drumbeat.

One of the men also carried a wooden cage with a live chicken that flapped and squawked. Lord, what were they planning to do—slit its throat and drip the blood on Camille's immaculate floor? He'd bet the health department would have something to say about that.

Moving to a position against the wall, Jordan tried to keep his expression neutral. He'd seen a lot of interesting sights in his four years on the police force, but this was one of the most…amazing. Maybe because of the setting. Here were six voodoo worshipers and their priestess in the middle of a charming little Cajun restaurant with potted ferns hanging from the ceiling, bentwood chairs, a vase of carnations in the center of each table, and old-time New Orleans photographs decorating the brick walls.

Odette glided farther into the room, swaying along with her dancers to the rhythm of the drums and bells.

"Welcome," she intoned as she looked around the room at the faces turned toward her. "I am pleased to see so many of the faithful with us tonight."

The faithful. Sure.

Some of the people ranged around the tables seemed eager or excited for the main event to begin. Others were obviously embarrassed. And at least one tourist looked as if he was thinking about bolting for the door. But his wife put a restraining hand on his arm and he settled down.

The dancers were a swirl of color and sound around the priestess as she raised her voice and said, "Voodoo is a religion of many traditions, many spiritual paths. We come together this evening to alleviate pain, to cast our vision into the future, to merge our souls with the great collective consciousness."

The drumbeat became more frantic, and the priestess approached the people at the tables, lifting her hands toward the ceiling.

"Up. Get up. Up! Join the celebration of life," she urged. Reaching for the hand of one of the elderly matrons, she led her out into the open area where the woman began to sway awkwardly to the rhythm of the drums and bells. A second old gal joined her. Then the others in the room were dragged into the thick of it.

The whole thing might have seemed funny, yet there was a kind of unsettling quality in the air, as if anything could happen.

Jordan glanced over at Camille, who had slipped behind the refreshment table. Probably a good move if you didn't want to get chicken blood on your clothing, he thought.

The priestess had taken the bird out of the cage and was holding it high as the poor thing flapped its wings.

Just then a noise from the other side of the floor caught Jordan's attention.

His head jerked toward the disturbance, and his hand went to his weapon. Then his eyes widened as he zeroed in on one of the civilians who had been shuffling around the floor. The man faltered, gasping for breath, his hands clawing the air.

He was heavyset, his graying hair plastered to his head and sweat soaking his white shirt. Even from the back, Jordan knew it was Spiro DeLyon.

The man grabbed for a chair, pulling it over, the wooden back clattering against marble tiles.

Someone screamed as DeLyon toppled forward, following the piece of furniture downward.

Chapter Two

A film of cold sweat bloomed on Camille's bare arms as she watched the scene unfolding in front of her.

This couldn't be happening. Not in her restaurant. It was all too horrifying and unreal.

On a muffled groan, Spiro DeLyon slid to the floor. Miss Lulu, who had been dancing beside her husband, screamed and went down on her knees, hovering over him.

In that instant, the drums and bells went silent, as though someone had slammed a door shut.

Jordan was across the room in seconds, taking charge, his voice booming into the sudden deafening stillness.

"Stand back. Give him air," he shouted as he knelt over the fallen man.

Camille was vaguely aware that Odette had dropped the chicken she'd been holding and that the now unattended bird was flapping around the room, squawking in fright.

Quickly Camille crossed to Jordan and DeLyon. The older man lay deathly still, his eyes closed and his skin gray.

"Let me help," Odette murmured as she swept down beside Jordan and the unconscious man.

"He needs CPR. You know how to do it?" Jordan asked.

"No."

"Then stay back." Briefly he whipped his head toward Camille. "Call an ambulance—and the police."

Her pulse was pounding so hard she felt as if she was going to faint. Digging her nails into her palms to steady herself, she gave Jordan a tight nod before turning and crossing rapidly to the phone at the hostess station.

After making the call, she looked across the room at DeLyon, hoping against hope that he'd be sitting up, groggy but on the mend. Instead, Jordan was leaning over him, expertly performing CPR.

A squawking noise to her right distracted her. She saw that one of the drummers had chased the chicken into a corner and was attempting to get it back into custody.

Her guests—including Miss Lulu—were watching the unfolding drama in shocked silence. Crossing to the woman, Camille put a gentle hand on her arm. "Come sit down. Let Officer O'Reilly take care of him. He's with the police, and he knows what he's doing."

Miss Lulu nodded and allowed herself to be led to a chair. Then at Camille's urging, the rest of the patrons finally returned to their seats.

Odette had drawn apart from the others, her body rigid and her gaze fixed in the distance as though her mind was far away.

It seemed forever before the paramedics swept into the room. After giving them a brief description of what had happened, Jordan got out of their way, then crossed to Camille. Touching her arm, he murmured, "Good job. Thank you for getting the onlookers calmed down.''

The light contact sent a shiver through her body.

''It gave me something to do,'' she answered, speaking around the lump that had formed in her throat. She kept her head down, because she was thinking how wonderful it would feel to have his arms around her right now, even when she knew how inappropriate that thought was. Officer Jordan O'Reilly was just doing his job, and she had no right to ask anything special of him.

She moistened dry lips. ''What about Mr. DeLyon?''

''I think we've lost him,'' Jordan answered. His words were clipped off abruptly as he swung to his right and started running across the room. She saw him bolt through the door into the kitchen area. He emerged half a minute later, muscling one of the priestess's male attendants back into the restaurant. The man's eyes were wide, his skin paler.

''Sit down,'' Jordan growled.

''I don't want to get involved, you know,'' the man muttered, looking from Jordan to Camille and back again.

''Everybody stays until we find out what happened,'' Jordan said in a firm voice.

''You ain't the boss of me. You ain't the police.''

''I'm afraid you're wrong,'' Jordan answered, pulling out his shield. ''I'm an off-duty cop. So sit down.''

The man gave him a dark look and sat, just as the paramedics wheeled DeLyon out of the room.

Jordan returned to Camille and gave her hand a quick squeeze. ''You're doing fine,'' he said.

''Am I? One of my customers is dead, and I can't help feeling it's my fault!''

His gaze sharpened. "You have some personal knowledge of what just happened?"

"Of course not. I just mean…I provided the venue for the ceremony."

He looked as if he was going to ask another question, but a moaning sound from nearby made them both turn. Miss Lulu was standing by the door, her shoulders shaking.

Both of them quickly crossed to her.

"I want to go with him," she sobbed. "But they told me I couldn't ride in the ambulance."

Jordan put a gentle hand on her shoulder. "They have to follow their rules. Is there someone who could take you?"

She turned toward Camille. "Can I call my sister?"

"Of course."

Camille led the sobbing woman to the phone, while Jordan addressed the rest of the group. "Thank you all for your cooperation," he said loudly. "A member of the detective division will be here to question you shortly. Meanwhile, I need everyone's name, address and telephone number. If you're a visitor to the city, include the name of your hotel."

One of the tourists stood up. "I protest being kept here. I had nothing to do with what happened."

Jordan turned toward him and said in a firm voice, "I'm sorry. I must insist on your cooperation."

"You're letting that other lady go!"

"Her husband is in that ambulance," Jordan snapped, giving the guy a hard look as he pulled out a notebook. "You want to join him?"

The man blanched and sat down, then lowered his head and began writing.

Camille breathed out a little sigh, profoundly grateful

that Jordan was handling the situation. If he hadn't been there, half the people would have bailed out by now.

Most of the patrons were finished writing the requested information when the door opened and another man wearing an obviously well-tailored pin-striped suit stepped into the room. Beside her, she heard Jordan swear softly as the newcomer crossed to him.

GREAT, JORDAN THOUGHT. *The icing on the cake. Gary Yancy.* He and the detective eyed each other with ill-concealed dislike, while Jordan mentally went through the short list of why he'd felt his stomach knot when the hard-assed detective had walked in the door.

He'd had more than one run-in with the bastard. Like the time Yancy had let him know that doing interviews wasn't his job.

The man had a chip on his shoulder, probably because other detectives had been promoted over him. Which wasn't going to make the next few hours very pleasant.

The little man strode into the room as if he was looking for trouble. Where was his partner? Rebecca Romero was a good cop, and she was usually able to keep a leash on the guy. But as far as Jordan could see, she wasn't in evidence. Too bad.

With an inward sigh, he stepped forward and gestured toward Camille. "This is Miss DuPree, the restaurant owner."

Yancy gave her a long look. "You one of the big-shot DuPrees?"

Her cheeks reddened. "I'm not sure how to answer that. If you mean, does my family have an interest in this restaurant, the answer is no. I started Camille's on my own, without any help from my relatives."

"The name can't hurt," Yancy countered.

"If I'd wanted to trade on the DuPree name, I would have put it in gold letters on the window," Camille answered. "But really, did you come here to talk about my business or to investigate a death?"

"Right," Yancy clipped out, then turned to Jordan. "Want to tell me what happened here?"

"A voodoo ceremony was in progress, and one of the participants keeled over and died."

"Voodoo!" Yancy zeroed in on Odette and her retinue before demanding more details from Jordan.

At the conclusion of the summary, he raised his voice and said, "Okay, I want everybody at the station for questioning."

Knowing they all had a very long evening ahead of them, Jordan stifled a sigh.

As CAMILLE COOLED her heels in a small room at the police station, her mind kept playing back the terrible events of the evening—and coming up with new questions. For instance, was she being accused of something?

Finally the door opened. When she saw a man in a blue uniform, her heart leapt. Jordan!

But it wasn't him, and she had to fight back her disappointment.

"This way, ma'am," the officer said, then escorted her down the hall to another small room.

As she stepped through the doorway, Yancy looked her up and down. Without being invited, she sat down in the hard wooden chair across the table from him.

"I'll want a list of all the dishes you served tonight and the ingredients in them," he said.

Camille felt her breath go shallow. "You think there was something wrong with my food?"

"One of your patrons is dead."

"Was…was he poisoned?"

"We'll know soon." The detective sounded as if he expected her to make a full confession.

As she looked into the rigid lines of his face, a terrible thought struck her. "Is anyone else sick?"

"Not so far."

"Thank God."

Yancy looked from her to the papers spread on the table in front of him and back again. "You had an illegal alien working in your restaurant."

"That's impossible. I document all my workers."

"One of Ms. LaFantary's drummers."

"I…I didn't know."

"You also exposed your patrons to a dangerous situation. A Voodoo ceremony!"

"Voodoo is a legitimate religion," she answered.

He laughed. "Yeah, and my mother is a prizefighter." He followed the remark with another loaded question. "So what is Ms. LaFantary paying you for the use of the restaurant?"

Did she have to answer that? Camille wondered. Maybe she should get a lawyer. But she hadn't done anything wrong. No, she could handle this herself.

After an hour of Yancy's interrogation, she was struggling to hold herself together. But finally the detective declared that she was free to go—as long as she remained in the city.

So worn-out she could hardly stay on her feet, she exited the building, determined that she wasn't going to fall apart.

She had answered endless questions about her business, about her patrons, her relationship with Odette and her handling of the emergency. And now she felt as limp as a failed soufflé.

Stepping into the humid darkness of the New Orleans June night, she grabbed the metal railing of the station-house steps to keep from swaying. When a steadying hand closed over her shoulder, she turned her head and saw Jordan standing beside her. Sometime during her time at the station, he'd changed out of his security company uniform and into civilian clothing—a dark T-shirt, light jacket, jeans and loafers. He looked strong and capable and very appealing. Unable to help herself, she leaned into him, and his arm slipped lower, holding her against his side.

"I'm sorry," he muttered.

"For what?"

"I'm sorry about DeLyon keeling over. And I'm sorry that bastard Yancy showed up. I know he gave you a hard time."

"Yes. First he acted like I poisoned Mr. DeLyon. Then he practically accused me of conspiring to destroy the crime scene. I tried to tell him the paramedics and my customers made a mess of the area. But he didn't want to listen."

"Paramedics go to specialized classes to learn how to destroy as much evidence as possible."

Despite everything, she laughed. "You're kidding, right?"

"Yeah. Well, only partly."

"Do you think Yancy was as hard on everybody else as he was on me?"

"Probably. He's got a chip on his shoulder the size of a Mardi Gras float."

Again she laughed. Jordan had always been able to

do that with her—make her see the lighter side of any problem.

She realized suddenly that he was studying her carefully. ''You're exhausted. Let me give you a ride home,'' he said.

She pulled herself up straighter, determined not to let old feelings lull her into making any mistakes. Marching down the steps, she headed toward the street. ''I'll get a cab.''

He caught up with her and steered her toward the parking lot. ''The hell you will!''

He'd been polite and professional up till that moment. Suddenly his words and the tone of his voice reminded her of another facet of the old Jordan O'Reilly.

He'd been angry about a lot of things back when they were in high school. He was angry now. And he could be dangerous when he thought someone was putting him down.

All that flashed through her mind. Still, when he turned her toward him, she didn't resist. She was shaky from the mean-spirited grilling Yancy had given her. Shakier still from the close contact with Jordan, from the immediacy of this man looming over her in the early-morning darkness.

When they were teenagers, she hadn't known what to expect from Jordan O'Reilly. He could change from cold to hot in the blink of an eye. She saw that in his face tonight. There was a charged moment when his green eyes bored into her blue ones, and she knew for certain that whatever had sparked between them all those years ago hadn't gone away. The knowledge gave her a jolt of satisfaction.

Still, he was older now. More controlled. Maybe he was silently asking her to tell him no. But that one simple syllable was beyond her power. Not when he was so close, so vital.

In unconscious invitation, she tipped her head to a more convenient angle, her lips parted.

She heard him swear. Heard him mutter something she didn't quite catch. Perhaps it was *I've been wanting to do this all evening.*

Or was that only what she *wanted* to hear?

As if the voodoo gods had brought her soul mate back to her on this fateful night, he lowered his head to hers. The first mouth-to-mouth contact was like a jolt of electricity, two opposite forces clashing, then merging, settling. Coming to terms.

It had been six years since she'd felt such a surge. Yet those six years were now wiped away as though they'd never existed. She knew only the heady taste of him, the taste of raw maleness and potency and hunger. She felt the strength of his arms, the heat of his body as he gathered her in.

The combination swamped her.

He made a deep growling sound that sent a hot glow to every nerve ending in her body.

She thought she remembered his kisses, his body. But she didn't remember this mastery, or this commanding presence.

He'd grown up in the years they'd been apart. Perhaps long ago she'd intimidated him. Now he had taken charge of the kiss, taken charge of *her.* When one of his hands slid down to her hips, pulling her lower body against his erection, she made a needy sound and moved in concert with him. They had done this before. And more. But they had always stopped before she could "get herself into real trouble," as her mother had put it.

Now she wanted desperately to know what making love with him would be like. And she wasn't sure what would have happened if he hadn't suddenly and abruptly ended the kiss.

They stood in the shadowy parking lot, staring at each other, breathing hard.

She felt wildly off balance. Had for hours. And because she was in pretty bad shape, words escaped her mouth before she had time to think about the consequences.

"Jordan, why did you walk away from me six years ago?"

Stunned silence hung heavy in the night air.

When he spoke, his voice was stiff and gravelly. "I wasn't the one who walked away."

"That's not how I remember it."

Again, his eyes burned into hers. "Does it matter?"

"Yes."

"No. You did me a favor. Or maybe it was the other way around. What really matters is that we're all wrong for each other. And I apologize for losing my head just now."

The apology was like a slap in the face. And she didn't want him to see the film of tears that suddenly clouded her vision.

Lowering her head, she started across the blacktop. He caught up with her and grabbed her arm. When she tried to wrench away, he held her in place.

"Neither one of us is in good enough shape for a personal encounter," he muttered.

"I know why I'm in bad shape. What's your excuse?" she asked, unwilling to admit she was still shaken by the kiss.

He chose to focus on police business. "You might

have noticed that Yancy and I don't get along very well. You weren't the only one he chewed up and spat out tonight.''

"Oh."

"If he catches us out here, he'll probably arrest us for illegal consorting.''

"You're kidding!''

"Yeah.'' He made a quick change of subject. "I don't want you going home alone. It's late and you're tired. That's a bad combination.'' As he spoke, he steered her toward an old Ford at the far end of the parking lot.

Perhaps because he was right, she let him open the passenger door. He reached across her to lift a folder from the seat, and she felt the brush of his arm across her middle like a small jolt of lightning. He must have felt it, too, because he drew back his hand like the snap of a whip. And she knew that whatever he might have said about being sorry, there was no denying the sexual awareness zinging between them.

She seated herself and he closed the door, then climbed behind the wheel and started the engine.

"You still live in the DuPree mansion?'' he asked.

"No. I wanted to be on my own. Maybe I should change my name. I could be Camille Smith. Would that make a difference to you?''

He answered with a grunt that she couldn't identify as yes or no.

"As a matter of fact, I live above the restaurant,'' she said.

"You're kidding.''

"I think you have a distorted view of my finances. My mother may live on her investment income—which, by the way, hasn't been so wonderful since the stock market plummeted. I inherited some money from my grandmother and I used all of it to equip Chez Camille. Until that mugging, I thought I was going to make it. Now I'm not so sure.''

"But you're a good cook!"

"How do you know?"

"I remember the goodies you used to make me. Your *pain perdu* was out of this world."

"It doesn't take much skill to make French toast."

"It was great. And your chocolate cake."

She cast him a sidelong glance. After all this time, he still remembered her teenage cooking.

He drove slowly down Burgundy Street, and she knew he was scanning the area for trouble.

"My door is around the side, in the courtyard."

"I'll go with you."

She suspected it would be useless to say she didn't need an escort, so she waited while he pulled up in front of the courtyard entrance. They trooped past her second-hand wicker furniture and potted hibiscus plants—an indulgence she hadn't been able to resist.

Jordan was in the lead, and when he got to her front door, he stopped short, a low curse springing to his lips.

Chapter Three

"What?" Camille was at his side, where he stood peering down at the object that lay on the doormat. It was dark and misshapen, with chicken feathers, a nail and other things sticking out of a solidified mass of goop.

When she saw what it was, she drew in a sharp distressed breath. "That…that looks like gris-gris, a voodoo charm. Bad magic."

Jordan pulled a small bamboo stick out of one of her flowerpots and used it to pick up the disgusting-looking lump. "Yeah. I know what gris-gris is. Maybe somebody can get fingerprints off the black goop. Do you have a plastic bag we can put it in?"

She opened the door and hurried up the stairs, stopping to unlock the door at the landing. In the kitchen, she got a plastic bag and brought it back to Jordan. Carefully he pushed the thing into the bag. Without asking if he could come in, he stepped through the door, then waited while she turned the lock behind them.

When they reached the living room, she watched him looking around at her cast-off family furnishings. She'd done her best to make the apartment homey, but she wondered how it would strike him. Then she canceled the silent question. What did it matter what Jordan O'Reilly thought of her decorating skills?

"Nice," he commented.

"Thank you," she answered, feeling some of the tightness in her chest ease.

He set the plastic bag on the coffee table, then walked around, closing blinds, darkening the room.

"What are you doing?" she asked, feeling as though he was shutting them off from the world.

"Making sure nobody can watch us from outside."

"Oh," she murmured, then caught her breath as Jordan turned from the window and they collided in the darkness in the middle of the room.

"Sorry," they both said at once.

Quickly she switched on a lamp with a beaded shade before settling into a wing chair. Jordan took the sofa and stretched out his long legs, crossing them at the ankles. But she could see from the set of his shoulders that he wasn't relaxed.

"What are you thinking?" she asked.

He swept his arm toward the voodoo charm. "That thing isn't exactly a Hallmark greeting card. It's a nasty warning. I don't like it. And I don't like the idea of your being here alone tonight. Whoever left that thing could be coming back."

"I think somebody's just trying to scare me," she answered, struggling to hold her voice steady.

"Are you willing to bet your life on that?" he countered.

She swallowed, then shook her head.

"I'm staying." His blunt statement made her breath catch. But before she could calm down, he followed up with another shocking remark. "Who are your enemies?"

She turned her palms up in a helpless gesture. "I didn't think I had any enemies. Well, there's that guy who tried to run out the door. You stopped him, but I could see he was angry with both of us. And Yancy said he was an illegal alien."

"You know his name?"

"I'll have to get it from Odette."

"What about her?"

"What do you mean?"

"She could blame you for DeLyon's death."

"Never!"

It looked as if he was taking the denial under advisement. Then he asked, "Okay, who else?"

She took her bottom lip between her teeth, then released it. "I guess I should mention my cousin Cort. He, uh, was angry that my restaurant was doing better than his. And he threatened to put me out of business."

"Oh, yeah?"

"He was upset. I don't think he meant it."

Jordan pulled out his notepad. "Give me his name and address."

When she'd done as he asked, he brought the questions back to Odette. "How did you end up letting a voodoo priestess use your restaurant for her nut-ball ceremony?"

"You think voodoo is a joke?" she shot back.

"No. I think it's real. And I think it's dangerous. I guess I phrased that wrong. What I really want to know is how you got involved."

She sighed. "The admissions fee brings in a thousand dollars a week. Sometimes more. Odette and I split it."

"How do you know her?"

"I met her through a lawyer friend."

"Well, tomorrow we're going to talk to her. Tonight we'd better both get some sleep."

"I've only got one bed," she said, then blushed as she thought of how that must sound.

"I can bunk on the sofa," he answered easily.

Struggling to keep her mind in neutral, she gave him a tight nod, then went down the hall to the linen closet to get a blanket.

JORDAN KICKED OFF his loafers, pulled off his jacket and set his gun, a Sig, on the coffee table before lying down on the blanket that Camille had spread over the sofa. He couldn't help wondering what his older brother, Liam, would think if he saw him now. He and Liam had both spent time hanging around the DuPree house during the fifteen years their mother had worked there. Liam had known he was stuck on Camille Du-Pree. He'd told Jordan to do something about it. Well, here he was—on her couch.

Pretty sure that he wasn't going to get much sleep, he tried to make himself comfortable as he listened to her making bedtime preparations. The bathroom was only a few feet away, and he imagined her in there, changing into a sexy gown. Then he canceled the thought. With him in the apartment, she was probably sleeping in her clothes, the same way he was.

Her bed must be right on the other side of the wall from the couch because he heard the mattress springs creak as she lay down, then creak several times more as she tried to get comfortable.

Maybe she was worried about who had left that nasty-looking bunch of gook and feathers outside her door. Or maybe she was as hot and bothered as he was.

He'd told himself a million times that he was better

off without Miss High Society DuPree. He'd almost convinced himself—until he'd seen her tonight looking just as beautiful and desirable as he remembered.

And that kiss. They'd both been off balance from Yancy's interrogation. But that couldn't account for the heat that had leaped between them when his mouth had touched hers.

Now, with only one thin wall separating them, his body was on fire. He wanted to make love with her. More than anything he'd ever wanted in his life.

They'd done plenty of hot and heavy fooling around, but he'd never been inside her. Well, only with two very lucky fingers. Now he ached to find out what the real deal would be like.

He grabbed two handfuls of the blanket and squeezed his eyes shut, trying to blot out his need for her. Nothing had really changed. He was still the hired help, and she was the princess in the ivory tower. Only, she wasn't really acting like a princess. He could see that she was working hard to make her restaurant a success and that she wasn't spending much on furnishing her apartment.

The restaurant location was another clue to the state of her finances. It wasn't exactly the best part of town. No wonder one of her patrons had been mugged. Or was that connected with this current case? Was De-Lyon's death somehow a deliberate attack on Camille? He was thinking about that when he heard a noise outside in the little courtyard.

It could be the paperboy, he supposed, making an early-morning delivery. If she even got the paper, which he didn't know. Slipping on his shoes, he grabbed his weapon, opened the door and tiptoed down the stairs.

He waited just inside the lower door, listening intently. Then he threw the door open and stood with the

Sig in a two-handed grip. Nothing looked out of place. But something in the air didn't feel right, and he'd learned to pay attention to his cop's instincts. So he took several more steps into the darkness.

Maybe he'd heard a stray cat, he thought as he started toward an exit from the patio that looked as if it probably led to the alley behind the restaurant. As he stopped in the archway, the sound of someone breathing warned him that he wasn't alone.

Chapter Four

Jordan started to turn just as something came down on the back of his head, quick and sharp. He managed a groan before he crumpled to the ground and everything went black.

He wasn't sure how long he was unconscious. The next thing he knew, he was waking up on the patio pavement with Camille bending over him. She had set a flashlight on the ground, and its beam cut through the darkness beside him.

Through slitted eyelids he noticed the light, but most of his attention was focused on the woman whose breasts were softly brushing his chest.

He wanted to reach up and cup one, but prudence kept his hand where it was.

"Jordan. Wake up! Jordan."

As she spoke, one of her palms stroked his cheek, a very pleasant sensation. He didn't mind drifting on that tender touch for another few moments.

Then he realized her other hand was pressed against his neck, probably checking his pulse, and he couldn't in good conscience let her keep thinking he was out cold.

"I am awake," he answered.

"Thank God."

His movements slow and deliberate, he reached up, caught her hand and folded his fingers around hers.

"Are you all right?" she asked, tightening her grip.

"Yeah," he answered automatically as he silently took a quick physical inventory. His head felt as if he'd been on a two-day drunk, but when he moved his arms and legs, everything seemed to be working.

When he started to sit up, pain lanced through his skull, and he thought better of changing his position—at least for the moment. "Did you see who coldcocked me?" he asked.

"No. I heard something outside. When I went into the living room, you were gone. I was standing at the top of the stairs, and then I heard you...heard you groan. Out here."

"You should have stayed inside."

"What was I going to do? Just leave you here?"

"No," he conceded. Figuring he might as well get it over with, he sat up, struggling to hold back a curse.

"Jordan!"

"I'll be fine." Gingerly he touched the back of his head and muttered something foul when his fingers came away sticky. He sensed Camille was watching him like a teacher on the lookout for cheaters. In the next second, the flashlight beam illuminated the red stuff he hadn't wanted her to see.

"You're bleeding!" she gasped.

"It's not serious," he answered, trying to put the best spin possible on the head injury.

"I should call an ambulance."

"No!"

"Jordan, you don't have to put on some kind of macho performance."

He sighed. "I'm not trying to be macho. But I'm in no shape for an argument, so I'll give my best evaluation of the situation. I already got chewed out by Yancy for moonlighting as a security guard at your voodoo ceremony. He hated that I was there as an off-duty cop. He'd just love to know I got hit over the head playing bodyguard. So let's go back inside and see how I do."

"Playing bodyguard?"

"That's the spin he'll put on it."

She hesitated for a moment, then answered, "Okay."

And he understood he was on probation.

Another very bad thought made its way into his fogged brain, and he cursed again.

"What?"

"My gun."

"I found it. Next to you. It's right here."

He thanked the voodoo gods for small favors. All he needed was to have to report that his Sig was missing.

After jamming the piece into the waistband of his jeans, he let Camille help him up and waited for several moments for his head to stop spinning.

Then, figuring he might as well enjoy himself, he allowed some of his weight to rest on her, in the process slinging his arm around her waist just under her breast.

He heard her draw in a quick breath, but she didn't pull away as they made their way back to her apartment entrance, where he reminded her to lock the door before they climbed slowly up the steps.

Her bare leg kept brushing against him, and he slid his eyes toward her, seeing that she was wearing a long T-shirt. Not a sexy gown as he'd imagined.

By the time they reached the top of the stairway, they were both panting. He wanted to sink onto the first available piece of furniture in the living room. Then he thought about getting blood on her upholstery and kept going until he reached the bathroom, where he sat down heavily on the closed toilet seat.

"I'm going to turn on the light," she warned.

He shut his eyes, then opened them enough to look at her through lowered lashes as she leaned over him to check his head. One of her breasts was practically in his face, and she wasn't wearing a bra. He could see the dark circle of the nipple right at eye level. Nice.

A jolt of pain brought him back to his senses. His curse had her scrambling to apologize.

"Jordan, I'm sorry. I was trying to see your wound."

"Yeah. How is it?"

"I don't know. I have to wash it off."

He let her do that.

"Well?"

"A lump and a small gash. I think you need stitches."

"Is it still bleeding?"

"No."

"Then forget the stitches. Just put some antiseptic on it."

When she finished, she drew back and met his eyes. "You should go to the hospital and—"

He cut her off. "I just need to lie down."

"On the bed."

He wasn't going to argue about that, but he grabbed a towel to make sure he didn't get any blood on her pillow.

He set the Sig on the bedside table, then lay down on top of the covers.

She'd climbed out of the bed only a short time earlier, and he allowed himself a few moments to enjoy the pleasure of being enfolded by her scent before asking, "You got that flashlight?"

"It's in the bathroom."

"You need to check my pupils to make sure they're contracting okay."

She scurried off to get the light, then did as he directed. The light hurt, but apparently he passed the test because she didn't try again to rush him off to the emergency room.

"You have to wake me up and do that every couple of hours," he said. "And I guess you'd better ask me if I know the date and what happened to me."

She gave a little nod.

"So you might as well lie down next to me," he added.

He saw her shift her weight from one foot to the other. "I can't do that."

"I'm harmless." He waited, his breath shallow. He wasn't thinking too straight, but he knew for sure that he wanted her in bed with him, and he figured he had a good excuse for asking.

He worked at keeping his breathing even as she climbed onto the mattress beside him. He wanted to reach for her, but he contented himself with easing his shoulder against hers. When she didn't move away, he slowly inched his arm over until the back of his hand was resting against hers.

It wasn't enough. He wanted to turn his hand over and clasp her fingers between his. But he wasn't going to press his luck.

As he drifted off, he let a little fantasy curl through his brain. A fantasy in which she turned to him in her sleep, and they ended up in a tangle of limbs in the morning.

TWICE DURING the remainder of the night, Camille checked Jordan's pupils and asked him where he was and why. Each time she breathed a sign of relief when he seemed to be okay.

She'd lain awake for hours before he'd been attacked. Now she was nervous about being in the same bed with him, but fatigue finally claimed her. Some time before sunrise she drifted off—then awoke to sensations she hadn't experienced in a long time.

She was lying on her side, pressed against a very hard male body. An aroused male body, she realized.

She lay there for several seconds, trying to keep her breathing even. But she heard Jordan swallow hard, and she realized he knew she was awake.

In the morning light she saw that he was looking at her, his face slightly flushed. He said nothing, but one of his hands slid down her body, cupping her hip and pressing her against him.

She made a small sound that was probably half protest. She couldn't be absolutely sure. She should move away. She knew that, on some esoteric intellectual level. But her body didn't seem to be in synch with good sense.

Closing her eyes again, she lowered her head to Jordan's shoulder, pressing her face against the soft fabric of his T-shirt, feeling his hot skin beneath.

She had wanted to make love with Jordan O'Reilly for as long as she could remember. And now he was in her bed. Obviously on the same physical wavelength.

She saw his hand move, felt it gently cup her breast, and a wave of need swept through her.

"Camille," he murmured. "That's so good."

"Yes."

One of her arms was trapped between them. With her

free hand she stroked the curve of his hip and down his leg, wishing she felt naked skin, instead of well-washed denim.

He gathered her closer, his arms circling her body. Rolling, she pressed him to his back and heard him groan.

A groan of pain, she realized, because she'd jammed his head against the pillow. Lord, what was she doing? He'd been hurt last night, and here she was acting as if he was perfectly all right.

She backed away from him, then sprang off the bed.

"I'm sorry," she managed.

He didn't speak for several seconds. When he did, his voice was gritty. "So you still think you're making a mistake getting tangled up with me."

"That's ridiculous."

"What then?"

"Jordan, you were knocked unconscious last night. You're…you're in no shape for doing anything in bed besides resting."

He sat up carefully. His movements were slow and deliberate, but his scowl told her he was still in pain.

"You and I need to talk," she murmured.

"About what?"

"About *us*."

"There is no us," he said in a voice that told her the conversation had ended.

She felt her vision blur. Apparently it didn't take much for him to get deep under her defenses and for him to show her his angry brittle side.

She didn't want him to know he'd hurt her. With her lips pressed together, she turned her back on him and pulled clean underwear from her dresser, then found a T-shirt and jeans. Wadding the clothing into a ball, she headed for the bathroom, where she showered and dressed in record time.

When she came back, she thought Jordan had left, and she felt a terrible sense of loss. Her mood bounced up immediately when he walked back into the apartment, carrying an overnight bag.

"I keep a change of clothes in my car. I hope you don't mind if I shower here," he said as though nothing personal had transpired between them.

"You could do that at home."

"I'm not leaving you alone until we find out who sent you that voodoo charm."

"You have to work, don't you?"

"I took some days off," he growled, then walked past her into the bathroom.

She was left standing in the living room staring after him. Well, if he could act so blasé, so could she. By the time he emerged from the bathroom, she had brewed a pot of hickory-laced coffee and was making omelets with onions, peppers and andouille sausage.

"That smells good," he said from the doorway as he set down his overnight bag.

She gave a tight nod.

"I'm sorry I'm in a grumpy mood," he added.

"I guess you're entitled," she answered. "Sit down and eat."

He sat. After setting plates and mugs on the table, she pulled out the chair opposite him.

He forked up a bite of the omelet, then chewed and swallowed. "This is really good."

"Thanks. That's what two years at the CIA will do for you."

His head jerked up. "The CIA?"

"The Culinary Institute of America."

He grinned. "You got me on that one." After another bite, he said, "I want to go over to Odette's shop with you. She may tell you things she won't tell the police."

"I'm not an absentee restaurateur. I have to go down and make sure my staff is on track."

He shifted in his chair. "Not for a few days. Yancy wants the restaurant closed until he's finished with the investigation there."

"You can't be serious."

"Sorry."

Her throat tightened. "Then I'd better call people so they don't show up for work."

She was fighting tears once more as she got out her phone book and started calling staffers. Some she was able to reach. With others, she could only leave messages.

In the middle of the phone calls, another thought struck her. Striding to the television, she got one of the morning newscasts—and was just in time to see Chez Camille's flash on the screen. The voice-over gave a lurid account of the voodoo ceremony and DeLyon's death. To top it off, at the end of the report there was a rehashing of the mugging incident.

"That's just perfect," she muttered when the topic switched to a barge collision on the river. "I guess I don't have to worry about Yancy closing me," she whispered. "Nobody will be coming, anyway."

Jordan moved up behind her and put his arm around her shoulders. "They'll come. They'll be curious. You'll get the same kind of tourists who attended the voodoo ceremony."

She supposed he was trying to make her feel better, but the observation didn't lift her spirits. Unable to accept his comfort, she held herself stiffly. "It looks like the dumbest thing I ever did was let Odette talk me into using the restaurant.''

"It was her idea?"

"Yes."

"Well, then, she owes you some answers to the questions I've got,'' he said, his voice hard-edged. She cut him a sideways glance. It sounded as if he cared about helping her. But there was no way to know for sure—not unless he was willing to open up about where they'd messed up six years ago.

By nine, they were out of the apartment. As she put a notice on the front door of the restaurant saying she'd be open again soon, she tried to ignore the curious stares of some of the locals who'd seen the police commotion. But Mr. Fitch from the antique shop a few doors down wouldn't allow her to escape without taking her to task.

He started the conversation with "I warned you that voodoo stuff was bad news.''

"I'm sorry you feel that way,'' she answered pleasantly.

"That Thursday-night bunch gave the whole neighborhood a bad name. Maybe now you'll cut out the funny stuff.''

Before she could reply, Jordan stepped between her and the antique dealer.

"Ms. DuPree has some business to attend to this morning. I'm sure she'd be happy to talk to you another time,'' he said.

"Yeah. And who are you? Besides the guy who shacked up with her last night.''

Chapter Five

Beside him, Jordan heard Camille suck in a sharp breath.

He hesitated a split second before saying, "I'm her fiancé."

He saw her head turn toward him, as though she couldn't believe what she'd just heard. Really, he hardly believed he'd said it himself. It had just slipped out of his mouth. When he took her arm, she let him lead her to the car and open the door, where she dropped like a stone into the passenger seat.

"Wh-why did you tell him that?" she stammered.

He'd spent the past thirty seconds trying to think of an answer. "What did you want me to say? That I'm a one-night stand?" he asked.

"No. That you're a cop, and you stayed the night to protect me."

He kept his eyes firmly on the road ahead. "You want *that* story to get out?" he asked. "I thought you were worried about your business. The bodyguard rumor gets spread around, and you lose a lot more customers."

He hoped that sounded plausible. He didn't know why the word *fiancé* had leaped to his lips. Maybe it had something to do with getting hit over the head. He still wasn't functioning at one hundred percent. But he was thinking well enough to realize that perhaps his long-buried yearnings had surfaced—despite his best efforts to deny them. Probably it had been a big mistake to kiss Camille outside the police station. But he hadn't been able to stop himself then, either.

He cast her a quick glance. She was sitting rigidly in her seat, staring straight ahead. He wanted to reach over and lay his hand over hers. He wanted to say he was sorry. He wanted to know how the princess of the DuPree family would feel about being engaged to him.

Instead, he cleared his throat and introduced a complete change of subject. "That guy Fitch given you trouble before?"

Camille clasped her hands in her lap. "Only verbal abuse."

"Would he go further than that?"

Her head swung toward him. "What do you mean?"

"Put rat poison in one of your customer's food?"

Her eyes widened. "Are you saying that's what happened to Mr. DeLyon?"

"We won't know until we get an autopsy report. Let's get back to Fitch."

"Mostly he's a windbag."

"So tell me about your cousin," he said, keeping the questions coming because he couldn't deal with anything more personal.

"Cort considers me a rival. I don't know why there's not room for both of us in New Orleans. I mean, the Brennan family has at least ten restaurants, and they all get along."

He collected some more information, then slowed as she gave him directions to Taboo. He convinced himself that he was feeling almost back to normal as he pulled into a parking space on Chartres Street.

But he was very conscious of Camille's hand dangling only a few inches from his as they walked to the shop. He wanted to grab that hand, stop her and pull her into one of the courtyards they passed.

But then what? What the hell was he going to say to her? That seeing her again had brought back feelings he'd told himself he'd exorcised from his soul?

He couldn't admit any of that, so he kept walking.

Taboo turned out to be a combination upscale beauty salon and voodoo boutique. The front, where the cosmetics were sold, was decorated in tones of peach and silver.

The colors in the back were deeper—red and gold, in keeping with the voodoo theme. On the shelves he could see several beautifully beaded boxes about the size of small hat boxes.

"Quite a setup," he commented.

"I think it makes the middle-class customers feel more comfortable playing around with voodoo," Camille told him. "You don't have to admit you're coming here for anything but face cream."

He caught the scent of exotic perfume. Then a curtain at the back of the shop parted, and a petite woman with very light café-au-lait skin, Caucasian features and a mop of dark curly hair stepped out.

Camille introduced her as Marie Germain, Odette LaFantary's new assistant, then asked if they could talk to the priestess.

"I'm sorry, she's not here." The woman looked down at her hands, then back at Camille. "Last night. That poor man. It was such a shock."

"Yes," Camille said.

"So where is Ms. LaFantary?" Jordan asked.

Marie gave a small helpless shrug. "She said she wouldn't be here this morning. She asked me to wait on anybody who came in."

Jordan studied her. She looked off balance. And he wondered if there was some way to push her. Did she have something to do with DeLyon's keeling over? Or last night's nasty calling card?

He held up the grocery bag he'd brought along, then turned it over and dramatically dropped the voodoo charm on the counter. It was still in its plastic-bag wrapping to keep outside fingerprints from contaminating the evidence. "We were hoping you could tell us something about this thing."

Marie blanched. "Where did you get that?"

Jordan watched her carefully. She was upset. But that didn't mean she hadn't had something to do with the damn thing.

"Camille found it on her doormat last night when she got home from the police station. We were hoping that Odette could tell us something about it. Since she's not here, maybe you have some insights?"

Marie picked up the bag and turned it one way and then the other, looking at the lumpy object inside.

"This is bad…" she murmured, then raised her eyes to Camille. "Whoever put it on the doorstep wished you ill. But it's not skillfully made. The person doesn't know a lot about the voodoo religion."

Or he or she was acting that way, Jordan thought.

"Can I keep this?" Marie asked.

Jordan opened his mouth to answer, when a voice from the doorway barged into the conversation.

"That thing is police-department property and it should be down at the station in the evidence room."

Everybody whirled around to find Detective Yancy watching them with narrowed eyes. He must have been there during most of the conversation, Jordan calculated. He wanted to curse aloud, but restrained himself. Still, he was pretty sure his face showed his state of mind—which was also the case with Yancy.

The detective looked him up and down. "I'll take that evidence," he said. "Did you have sense enough not to get your fingerprints on it?"

"I didn't touch it," Jordan answered, making an effort to keep his voice even. "And I was going to bring it in just as soon as we talked to Odette about it."

"Asking questions is my job, not yours. So I'd appreciate it if you kept your nose out of my investigation."

"This thing wasn't at the restaurant. It was at Ms. DuPree's house last night."

"It's still relevant, and you know damn well you should have called me."

Jordan wanted to say that it had been pretty late when they'd found the charm. But he could see there was no use getting into a pissing match with Yancy. The detective outranked him, and if he was going to do any further investigating, he'd have to proceed carefully.

Yancy was studying the two of them, and Jordan couldn't help feeling like a murder suspect about to be confronted with a startling revelation.

"I dug a little into your background," he said to Jordan in a conversational tone. "Apparently your mom cleaned the DuPree house."

"That's not a crime."

"So did you know each other when you were growing up? Did Mrs. O'Reilly cart her little boy to work with her in the DuPree mansion?" he asked.

"Sometimes," Jordan answered. "If you want more information, you can bring us down for a formal interview."

"I may do that," Yancy answered.

"Ms. DuPree and I were on our way out," Jordan said, taking Camille's arm.

"Ms. DuPree? That's kind of distant, isn't it, considering you spent the night together?"

Jordan's mouth went dry. "Our personal relationship is private," he managed to say.

"Nothing is private in a murder investigation," Yancy answered, making it sound as if they were involved in some kind of conspiracy.

"So is it a murder investigation? Did you get the coroner's report?"

"I don't have to share that information with you."

"Right."

Jordan steered Camille out of the shop and down the sidewalk. They didn't speak until they were back in the car.

"What's wrong with that guy?" Camille asked.

"He's desperate to close a big case," he answered as he pulled away from the curb.

"It sounds as if he's trying to pin a murder on us."

"Yeah. Too bad he discovered us together this morning. And too bad he talked to Fitch," he added, wondering if Camille's neighbor had mentioned that the happy couple who'd spent the night together claimed to be engaged.

Instead of pulling up in front of her restaurant, he drove around the corner so he could park in the alley in back.

When he glanced at Camille, he saw she had unhooked her seat belt and was gazing at him, her lips slightly parted.

Even though he knew it was a stupid move, he wanted very badly to kiss her. Just to prove he could do it without going up in smoke, he unhooked his own seat belt, bent and brushed her lips with his.

It was like an old-fashioned kitchen match striking wood. Heat flared, burning through his resolve.

He gathered her to him, deepening the kiss, angling his head to drink in everything he could from this woman he had wanted for what seemed like centuries.

She could have pulled away. Instead, she moved closer, her arms creeping around his neck as she kissed him with equal fervor. He wanted to pull her onto his lap, wanted to make love with her. Right now. Right here.

Instead, he forced himself to lift his head, staring into her eyes as they both struggled to drag in full breaths.

"Come inside," she murmured.

Chapter Six

Jordan couldn't stop himself from nodding. It was as if they had come to a silent agreement and now they were sealing the bargain. With fingers that felt as if they were covered with workman's gloves, he managed to open the car door. Quickly he came around to Camille's side of the car. When she wobbled on unsteady legs, he caught her to him.

Together they swayed into the courtyard, then up the stairs, stopping to caress and kiss each other as they ascended the long flight.

It appeared she had put her trust into his hands. And he didn't know whether he was worthy of that trust. Still, he found himself bending toward the front of her T-shirt, stroking the sweet curve of her breasts with his face, then turning to brush the hardened tips with his lips.

He'd touched her before. Her body was familiar to him. They'd done everything together except have intercourse. Neither one of them had been ready for that. So they'd brought each other to climax with hands and lips.

Six years ago that had been enough. Now he knew it

wouldn't satisfy him. Maybe she felt the same way, because she knit her fingers with his and led him to the bed they'd shared for a few hours the night before.

They tumbled together onto the mattress, even as he reached under her shirt and stroked the hot skin of her back before unhooking her bra.

She helped him get rid of it, and her shirt, so that he could swirl his tongue around one nipple, then suck it into his mouth.

''Oh, Jordan,'' she gasped, her hands plucking at his jacket and shirt.

He sat up, discarding his jacket and shoulder holster on the floor before dragging the shirt over his head so that he could clasp her to him, then groaned as he felt her naked breasts flatten against his chest.

His hands stroked the silky skin of her back and shoulders. He had no right to ask anything from her. But fate had brought them together again, and he couldn't stop from gasping out, ''Camille, I need—''

''Yes. Everything we can give each other.''

She struggled out of her jeans and panties while he got rid of his remaining clothing, then pulled her back into his arms, overwhelmed by the feel of her naked flesh against his.

Reverently he slid his lips along the tender place where her hair met her cheek, dipping down to nibble along the line of her chin and then the side of her neck, feeling her arch into his touch.

He was ready to make love. He had never been more ready. Yet he ached to make her feel what he was feeling.

His head dipped back to her breast, taking one nipple into his mouth and drawing on it while his hand found its mate, using his thumb and finger to gently stroke and tug, building her pleasure with all the skill and care he had ever possessed, using his knowledge of her body and what he had learned in the years since they'd been together.

All his senses were tuned to her, to the tiny sounds she made and the ripples of sensation that flowed across her body.

His free hand slid over her abdomen, then lower, finding the hot quivering core of her. Her hips moved against his hand as she silently told him how much she wanted him.

His own blood was boiling. He had never needed a woman more urgently, more violently.

Fighting the urge to conquer, he left the final decision to her. He rolled to his back and looked up at her.

She leaned over for a long deep kiss, then raised her head so she could look down at him as she straddled his hips.

The breath froze in his chest as he felt her lower her body to his, felt the intimate clasp of her sex around his, and he knew that this moment had been worth waiting for.

"Ah, Camille," he gasped as she began to move above him, around him.

She was so beautiful and sexy, her breasts thrust toward him, her eyes locked with his, as she started with controlled movements. But the pace quickly become more urgent, more demanding.

She took them both higher and higher, and his hand pressed to her center to intensify her pleasure.

"Oh, Jordan, Jordan," she said breathlessly, her movements becoming frantic as she sought her release.

Suddenly she cried out, her voice high and glad, just as his own body convulsed. They were swept along together in a great wave of pleasure.

He was left gasping for breath as she collapsed against him in a damp heap.

Long moments passed before either of them stirred. Then she shifted onto the bed beside him.

He stroked her arm. He wanted to tell her what making love with her had meant to him. But he'd never been great with words. So he simply continued to stroke her, hoping he might convey his feelings through his fingertips.

She turned her head and kissed his shoulder, and he sensed that she wanted to say something.

"What?" he murmured.

She hesitated, then asked in a barely audible voice, "Jordan, why didn't you answer my letters when you went away to your uncle's?"

CAMILLE KNEW the moment she'd asked the question that it had been the wrong time. And probably the wrong place.

Jordan sat up, staring down at her. "What?"

Reaching for the sheet, she carefully pulled it over her naked body and sat up before saying, "I wrote to you. But you never answered me."

He looked totally confounded. "No. You were the one who didn't write. I was a long way from home and I missed you so much. But you didn't answer me. And when I called your house, your mother said you weren't home."

She shook her head in confusion, trying to rearrange her thinking.

"I called and I wrote you," he repeated, punching out the words. "Then when I came home, you'd left for school in the East." Perhaps he was reacting to the dumbfounded look on her face when he said, "What? Do you think I'm lying?"

"No," she whispered. She'd been feeling so wonderfully relaxed and so close to him that she'd thought they could talk. Or maybe she was desperate for answers, because she kept asking him versions of the same question.

Too bad she'd acted without thinking when they'd come to her bedroom. Both of them had. Overcome by a rush of feeling, they'd plunged ahead into something that neither one of them was actually ready for. But she wasn't going to say she was sorry that she'd made love to him.

She watched him climb out of bed and start looking for the clothing he'd tossed on the floor.

While he was dressing, she got up and pulled on her T-shirt and jeans, then backed toward the door, trying to figure out what had just happened between them. The lovemaking had been glorious, but why had he done it? Because he'd seen the chance to get what she'd denied him all those years ago? She wanted to flee. But this was her apartment, not his.

Apparently he was having the same reaction. "I should go."

She answered with a tight nod.

"I don't feel comfortable leaving you alone."

"I don't need a baby-sitter!" she shot back.

"I'm not suggesting you do. But I have to know you're safe. Is there someone you could stay with for a few hours?"

She made an effort to bring her emotions under control. "I think I could go to Simone's," she said. "She's a lawyer. With her own practice."

"Simone Jones?"

"You know her?"

"I've seen her around the station. She's a pretty aggressive lawyer."

He didn't elaborate and she didn't press him. "She's the person who introduced me to Odette at that businesswomen's meeting," Camille volunteered.

"Oh, yeah? Is she into voodoo? Or was she hired to get Odette out of trouble?"

"She's always kind of been interested in voodoo." Cutting off the conversation, she reached for the phone and called Simone to make sure that hanging around her office for a few hours would be okay. Then she and Jordan got back into his car, where she sat with her hands knit together. Not so long ago, they had been passionately kissing here. Then they'd gone upstairs and finished what they'd started. She'd never been the kind of woman to make quick decisions about sex. But it had seemed so right. It had seemed right all the way up until she'd asked him a question about the past.

Now she wished she'd kept her mouth shut, although she knew that would only have postponed the reckoning.

"You want to ask her about Odette?" she inquired as he pulled into a no-parking zone in front of Simone's office. It was in the central business district, or the CBD, as the natives called it.

"I have some other stuff to do," he replied, "so I'll let you do that. And I'll come back for you in a couple of hours."

She had vowed not to ask any more questions. Unfortunately it seemed every sentence that came out of her mouth was in that form.

"Where are you going?"

"To have a chat with your cousin Cort DuPree."

She might have protested, but she knew that Jordan was going to follow his own agenda no matter what she thought about it.

So she exited the car, vividly aware of his eyes on her back as she walked toward the building.

Inside, Simone's secretary ushered her right into the office.

Her friend was sitting behind her desk, wearing one of her tailored suits, with a miniature Mardi Gras mask pinned to the collar. Her shoulder-length blond corkscrew curls bounced as she jumped up and embraced Camille.

"Oh, honey, I'm so sorry about last night. I feel kind of responsible."

"It's not your fault! Letting Odette use my restaurant seemed like a good idea at the time."

"I heard it on the news this morning. Was that man murdered?"

Camille's face contracted. "We don't know yet why he died. Jordan will tell me as soon as he finds out."

"Jordan?"

Camille felt a rush of heat to her face. "Jordan O'Reilly."

"One of the O'Reilly boys."

"You know them?"

"Just from work. They both seem like button-down cops. And we've been on opposite sides in a couple of cases." Simone switched the subject abruptly. "Their mom used to work for your folks, didn't she?"

"Yes. So I know him from way back," Camille answered, then hurried on. "He's been moonlighting for the security company I hired after one of my customers was mugged. He was on duty when DeLyon collapsed. Now Detective Yancy is giving him a hard time."

"Yancy is a real bastard. But his partner, Rebecca Romero, is okay. Let's hope you get to deal with her, instead of him."

Camille nodded. She didn't want to continue with the conversation, so she said, "I hardly got any sleep last night. Is there somewhere I can lie down?"

"Yes. I've got a hideout in the back where I catch a power nap when I'm working late. You're welcome to use it."

"Thanks. I appreciate this."

JORDAN WAS BACK at the lawyer's office a few hours later. The strained look on Camille's face made him want to pull her into his arms. With an effort, he simply escorted her to the car, then waited while she buckled her seat belt.

"What did Cort have to say?" she asked as they pulled away from the curb.

"What I expected. That he doesn't like you muscling in on his restaurant business. But he wouldn't have done anything to sabotage you."

"Did you believe him?"

"No. But I think I got him worried enough that he'll be afraid to pull anything."

"Well, right now he's got his wish. The restaurant is

closed,'' she said as he came to a stop in the alley parking space.

He gestured toward the door. "You can get back in tomorrow morning."

Her head swung toward him. "How do you know?"

"I made it my business to find out," he answered, unwilling to tell her that he'd risked Yancy's wrath to get the information.

"Thank you." She dragged in a breath and let it out—and he waited with his own breath held for whatever it was she was going to lay on him.

Chapter Seven

"I appreciate your watching out for me last night. And today. But I have to get my life back in order."

"Which means?" Jordan asked carefully.

"Like I told you. I don't need a baby-sitter."

"Okay," he agreed, trying not to sound too relieved.

She gave him a considering look, then thanked him again as she climbed out of the car.

He watched her until she was out of sight. She might think that he was going to let her fend for herself, but that was sure as hell not true. He was going to be around here, watching her place. And his older brother, Liam, had agreed to spell him. Together they would make sure nobody else came after her.

From a distance. Because he wasn't going to give in to temptation again the way he had this afternoon. He'd had no business climbing into bed with her. As far as he was concerned, he'd taken advantage of a woman who was emotionally off balance.

Now he had his priorities straight. That was what he told himself. He didn't dwell on the fact that he'd let all the old feelings for her surface again.

She'd rejected him once—or at least he thought she had. Now she was acting as if he was the one who'd

done it. Had he been wrong? Had the relationship somehow gotten derailed because of some colossal misunderstanding?

He hated to think that was true. And he hated to set
himself up to get hurt again. So backing off was the
right thing to do, as far as he was concerned.

CAMILLE WAS GLAD to be able to focus on work once
again. She knew time on her hands would only leave
her free to think about Jordan—a subject she wanted to
avoid.

As he had predicted, the police allowed her to reopen
Chez Camille the next morning. And a television re-
porter asked her to do an interview on the six-o'clock
news.

She hated interviews, wanting to showcase her cooking, not herself personally. But she agreed, because it
gave her the opportunity to tell the public she would be
open for business that evening.

Jordan was right. People were curious about the story
of the guest who'd collapsed during the voodoo ceremony. That night she had more customers than on any
Saturday in memory. And she was up early in the morning, down at the wholesale markets buying produce,
meat and fish for Sunday.

The crush continued. Every table was filled, and she
was taking reservations way into the next month.

But the biggest gratification came from the comments
diners were making when she stopped by their tables to
see if they were enjoying the food. Everyone she talked
to raved about her combination of Cajun specialties and
down-home Southern cooking. Several even suggested
that she publish a cookbook.

The praise didn't turn her head. She was smart

enough to know that it would take more than a few weeks of notoriety to firmly establish Chez Camille in a town full of good restaurants.

But it looked as if success was in her grasp.

Thankful that Tuesday was her day off, she took a nap in the afternoon. Then she decided she might as well use the time to bake some of her special sweet-potato pies.

She was in the restaurant kitchen alone, just after dark, when she heard a trash can rattle in the alley.

Her gaze shot to the window, but the darkness totally obscured her view. Still, if somebody was out there, she could definitely be seen.

Feeling a little foolish, she got out a butcher knife and laid it on the stainless-steel counter beside her workstation. The noise wasn't repeated, so she went back to mashing the sweet potatoes she'd just baked.

But her ears were tuned toward the door and window, and a few minutes later, she heard a noise again. It sounded as if somebody was trying to turn the lock. Suddenly she remembered that she'd gone out a little earlier. Had she forgotten to lock the door again?

Grabbing the knife, she prepared to defend herself from whoever was out there. Then the door burst open, and her eyes widened in shock as her cousin Cort came flying into the room. Jordan was right behind him, holding on to Cort's belt and hair.

"What?" she gasped, almost choking on the strong smell that had accompanied the men into the room.

"This jerk was in back of your restaurant dousing your trash with lighter fluid. I got to him before he committed arson."

"Let go of me!" the captive sputtered.

Instead, Jordan gave the man a hard shake, then spun

him around and pressed his back against the commercial refrigerator.

"Tell the lady what's going on," he demanded.

Cort must have seen the fire in Jordan's eyes. "Don't hurt me," he whined.

"You want to keep your nice pretty face, you explain why you were out there getting ready to torch her restaurant."

Cort folded his arms across his chest. "Because she got on TV a couple of days ago," he growled. "I thought she was finished when that DeLyon guy keeled over. But no. She's back in business—and doing better than ever."

"And that upset you?" Jordan prompted.

"You bet it did. I've been working my butt off getting customers. Getting restaurant reviews. Getting noticed. And she waltzes into town and starts taking my customers away."

"That's not what I intended," Camille protested.

"Well, that's what happened."

"So you arranged to have one of her diners mugged," Jordan said.

"I—"

Jordan gave him another shake.

"All right. Yes. I did."

"You bastard. You've been watching her apartment. And her restaurant."

"Not all the time. I have a business to run."

"Oh, right." Jordan snorted. "Did you slip something into Spiro DeLyon's drink?"

"Of course not! I wouldn't kill anybody."

"You could have killed Camille tonight."

"No. She would have seen the smoke and flames and gotten out."

''Sure. She's a regular fire warden.'' Jordan regarded him with a murderous expression on his face. ''What else did you do? Besides trying to start that fire. And arranging for the mugging. Did you leave a voodoo charm on her doorstep?''

''No,'' Cort said, but the denial lacked conviction.

''You did, didn't you?'' Jordan gave him yet another hard shake.

''I want my lawyer.''

Jordan swore. ''You're slime.''

''I want my lawyer,'' Cort repeated.

''Of course.'' Jordan read him his rights, then turned to Camille. ''I'm taking him down to the station. Even if he's the one who left that charm, I want you to go back to your apartment and lock the door. Don't let anyone in.''

''Yes. All right.''

Jordan hustled Cort out, and she was left trying to cope with everything that had just happened. She looked around at the kitchen. Quickly she cleaned up, her mind whirling. Cort had been harassing her. More than harassing, if he'd hired that mugger and planned to set her trash on fire.

He'd been the source of a lot of her problems. But there was another implication to what had just happened—Jordan had been right there. She'd told him she didn't need a baby-sitter, and he'd agreed. But he'd been watching out for her, anyway.

She clenched and unclenched her fists. She needed to talk to him. Was he coming back later?

JORDAN HAD TOLD Camille not to let anyone in. But when she heard a knock at the door two hours later, she jumped up and ran to look out the peephole, hoping it was him.

Instead, she saw Odette standing on the landing.

"I need to talk to you," the voodoo priestess said, addressing the one-way circle of glass that Camille was looking through.

Camille hesitated for a moment. She and Odette had been friends. But she had no idea how things stood between them now. After a silent debate, she turned the bolt and opened the door.

Odette had been a formidable figure on Thursday night in her white priestess outfit. She was still formidable in a striped dress that flowed around her legs and a pair of platform shoes that added several inches to her already considerable height.

"Thank you for letting me in," she said as she sailed into the apartment.

Camille backed up until her legs hit the edge of an easy chair, where she sat. "We tried to talk to you a few days ago," she said.

"I felt it was better to keep out of everybody's way." Odette took the chair opposite Camille. "If that man dropped dead during my ceremony, then I've got to be the prime suspect."

"The other morning at your shop, Detective Yancy acted like that was Jordan—or me," Camille managed.

"He's a real sweetheart."

Camille nodded. "Can I get you anything?"

"No need to play hostess. I came to bring you something." She reached into her large straw purse and pulled out something wrapped in pink tissue paper. When she unfolded it, Camille saw a silk bag about three inches thick and four inches wide, lightly filled with something. The top was closed with a gold ribbon.

Various beads and other small objects hung off the bottom of the bag or were sewn to the sides.

Camille stared at the object, which Odette laid on the coffee table. "It's pretty. But what…what is it?" she asked.

"A special charm."

When Camille looked skeptical, the priestess rushed on, "I know you don't believe in all that voodoo stuff, even though you let me hold those Thursday-night sessions. But you don't have to be a believer for it to work. I've been asking for help from the *loa*—the gods. This morning they told me you need this charm, so I'm leaving it with you."

"What is it? A love potion?" Camille asked, crossing to the coffee table and picking it up. It felt very light in her hand.

"Do you need a love potion?"

She gave a nervous laugh. "Maybe."

"Well, perhaps that's what it will turn out to be."

"You don't know?"

"People come to me for aid and comfort, and I do ceremonies or make them charms. But when the gods tell me what to make, I can never be sure about the outcome. Maybe this is to ward off Detective Yancy."

"Well, I could use that, too," Camille conceded.

"I'll leave you, then."

"Wait."

The priestess cocked an inquiring eyebrow.

"I wanted to ask you about that man. The one who tried to run out after Mr. DeLyon collapsed. Do you think he had something to do with what happened?"

"He's from Haiti. It turned out that his work permit wasn't in order. Yancy turned him over to the INS."

"Oh, I'm sorry."

"He knew he was taking a chance working for me."

"You were taking a chance, too."

"Not that big a one." Odette gave Camille a direct look. "I'm sorry that letting me use your restaurant got you into trouble. Well, it got both of us into trouble actually."

"It may turn out all right. I've got lots of people coming in because they're curious. They end up liking my food."

"I'm glad to hear it." Odette smiled. "You're like me. I think you will land on your feet."

After making that pronouncement, Odette turned toward the door. Moments later, she was gone.

And Camille was left with the charm her friend had brought. It lay where Odette had put it on the coffee table. Being alone in the same room with it made her feel funny. Intending to put the decorated bag into a drawer, she reached for it. The moment her fingers closed around the silky fabric, she felt a warm tingling sensation flood her hand.

With a shocked gasp, she tried to drop the charm, but her fingers simply wouldn't open.

Chapter Eight

"No!" Camille cried. But it was as if the thing had taken control of her body. The strange sensation in her hand spread up her arm, then through her. Knees suddenly weak, she dropped onto the sofa and leaned back against the cushions, trying to drag in air.

The room around her swam and blurred. She knew her body was still sitting there on the couch, but her mind was somewhere else. At first she felt as if she was in an endless dark place where she couldn't catch her breath. Then suddenly she was standing in front of her house. Not this apartment, but the Victorian mansion in the Garden District where she'd grown up.

Somewhere in her mind, she knew she wasn't really there. She couldn't be. But it felt amazingly real. The view seemed to be from the sidewalk just outside the wrought-iron fence.

It was spring, she could see, because the azaleas along the front of the property were in full bloom. But they were smaller than they looked now.

As she watched, her mother came out, and Camille stared, momentarily disoriented. Her mother was different, too. She appeared younger and more vigorous than she had in a long time, and Camille finally realized that she was seeing her not as she was now but as she had been some time in the past.

In fact, she knew it was the past because the old Mercedes was in the driveway, and her mother had sold that car five or six years ago.

In the vision, her mother marched down the steps and headed for the mailbox. Camille felt as if she was standing only five feet away.

"Mom," she called.

Her mother stopped short and glanced up, looked straight at Camille. But it was apparent she couldn't see her.

After pausing for a long moment, she went to the mailbox, opened it and took out a pile of envelopes, magazines and advertising circulars.

Most of the envelopes were business-size. One was smaller. And when her mother came to it, she stopped.

Camille moved closer and made a small astonished sound when she saw it was addressed to her. The name on the return address was Jordan O'Reilly.

Her mother paused and looked up, an expression on her face that was a mixture of anger and maybe guilt. Her fist closed around the envelope, crumpling it. In the next moment, she stuffed the letter into her pocket, then marched back to the house.

The scene around Camille started to fade—and she tried to hold on to it with a kind of frantic desperation. She wanted to know more. She had to know more. But the effort was wasted. Again, the charm seemed to have control of her. Suddenly she was back in her own living room, gasping for breath.

Involuntarily her hand opened, and the charm dropped to the rug. Staring down at it, she tried to catch her breath—and to figure out what had just happened.

She'd picked up the thing and it had transported her back in time. To her old house. And she'd seen her mother doing something that she couldn't believe.

Yet she'd witnessed it.

Was it real? Had she interpreted what she'd seen correctly, or had the charm made her only imagine something?

She had to know the truth. Now. Right this minute.

Glancing at the clock, she saw that it was almost midnight. But her mother had never gone to bed early. Now that she was older, she needed even less sleep. Camille knew that she could call her on the phone, but then she wouldn't be able to see her mother's face when she asked the question that now burned inside her.

Ignoring Jordan's instructions again, she grabbed her purse and hurried out of the house. In the alley she climbed into her car, then roared into the darkness.

She slammed to a stop in the driveway of the house where she'd grown up, then sat for several moments, breathing in and out and trying to get control of herself. Her emotions were running high, but it would be a mistake to frighten her mother by barging in unannounced so late at night. So she rang the bell at the front door. Then, because she also knew there was a button to activate the intercom from the outside, she turned the speaker on.

"Mom, are you there? I need to come in and talk to you."

"Camille? What are you doing here?"

"I need to ask you some questions, Mom."

"At this hour?"

"Yes. Where are you?"

"In the garden room."

Camille let herself in, then headed for the back of the

house, to the glassed-in conservatory where her mother loved to sit—even late at night.

In the darkness, it was impossible to see the beautifully landscaped backyard. But inside the conservatory, her mother sat in a comfortable wicker chair surrounded by a small palm and large ficus trees, their foliage illuminated by a glow of yellow light. Her gray hair was in a neat French twist, the way she'd been wearing it for the past forty years. As always, not a strand was out of place.

Mom had phoned after DeLyon's death hit the news, and Camille had assured her everything was all right. That was the extent of their conversation about the problem.

Now her mother closed the copy of *Architectural Digest* she'd been reading and studied her daughter with appraising eyes, apparently reading the distress on her face. "That voodoo priestess got you into trouble. I knew she would. I told you the restaurant market was overcrowded. I said that you and Cort should go in together."

"Mom, Cort tried to ruin me!"

"He wouldn't do that. He's a nice boy. And he's your uncle Jacques's son."

Camille sighed. Her mother had always had strong opinions. And she'd been good at ignoring details she found inconvenient.

"Well, Jordan O'Reilly arrested him. Cort was trying to burn the trash in back of my restaurant. And he arranged for that mugging a few weeks ago."

"Jordan? What's he got to do with this?"

"Cort made a lot of trouble for me, and Jordan discovered what he was doing. He kept Cort from burning down my restaurant."

"I don't believe it! That boy never knew his place. He's making it up."

"No, he's not. I was there. I saw what happened. I smelled the lighter fluid Cort had poured into my trash cans."

"I never wanted you mixed up with that O'Reilly boy," her mother continued as though Camille hadn't spoken.

Camille's eyes glittered as she advanced on her mother. "That's right. So you broke us up when his mom sent him to his uncle's in Baton Rouge to get him away from the rough crowd he was hanging out with here. You hid the letters he sent me. And you didn't mail the ones I sent him."

A flush spread across her mother's cheeks. "How do you know that? Did Dora say something to you?"

"Jordan's mom was in on it?"

"Dora does what I tell her to do."

Camille made a very unladylike exclamation. "Well, that's just great!"

"It was for the best. You didn't need that loser."

"He's not a loser. He's a hardworking police officer." Before her mother could say anything else, she turned and stomped out of the room and out of the house. She didn't start crying until she'd locked herself in her car. She let the tears flow for five minutes, then pulled herself together. She and Jordan had lost so much time. Now she had to tell him why. But she didn't have his phone number. She'd left the card he'd given her at home.

Quickly she retraced her route and pulled up in the alley in back of her house once again. Intent on calling Jordan, she charged up the steps. But when she rushed to the phone, she found that the light was blinking on her answering machine. Hoping it was Jordan, she pressed the button.

To her disappointment, it was the voice of Sadie Marceau, the portly older woman who attended Voodoo Night with her sister and friends.

"Camille! Where are you at this time of night? I just thought of something I need to tell you about…about what happened on Thursday night. I don't want to talk about it over the phone. And I don't want this getting back to that nasty Detective Yancy. So don't call me back. Please come to my house as soon as you get home."

JORDAN WAS just leaving the station house when his brother, Liam, came on shift. Liam had also followed in their father's footsteps and joined the force. So had their half brother, Zachary Doucet, for that matter. He caught a glimpse of Zach now, and nodded. Zach was a mistake his dad had made when he should have known better. The three brothers knew each other of course. They'd even shared a few meals. But they weren't exactly friends.

"You still need me to watch Camille's house?" Liam asked.

"I caught her cousin getting ready to set her trash cans on fire. And I'm also certain he's the one who left that voodoo charm outside her door."

"So the emergency is over."

"I think so. But I want to make sure. Do you mind being available for a few more nights if I need you?"

"I'm glad to do it. And I'm glad you and Camille got back together," his brother said. "I always wondered why the two of you broke up."

Jordan might have given his old standard answer—

because she didn't want me. Now he'd started wondering if it was really true. The problem was, when Camille
had tried to talk to him about it, he'd been too proud
to continue the conversation, because her old rejection
was still a festering wound. At least he could admit that
much.

"She and I aren't exactly back together. It just turns
out I was at her restaurant when all hell broke loose."

"And you asked me to help you guard her."

"Yeah, since she didn't want me staying in her apartment," he snapped.

"You're making a mistake letting her go."

"Do I have a choice?" Jordan asked.

"Come on. You know you do. Don't let that old
O'Reilly pride get in your away," Liam said, then
turned and walked to his patrol car, leaving Jordan
standing in the parking lot.

When he saw Gary Yancy get out of another car and
head toward him, he fought the impulse to cut and run.

"You've been poking your nose into the DeLyon
case again," the detective said by way of greeting.

"I want to make sure nothing else happens to Ms.
DuPree."

"Well, isn't that nice of you," Yancy answered with
a note of sarcasm.

"What's that supposed to mean?"

"Anything you want it to mean," the detective
snapped, giving him a long look before heading into the
station.

CAMILLE GLANCED at her watch. It was after midnight
now—pretty late to be going over to Sadie's. And the
idea of charging off into the night again set her nerves
on edge. Probably she should call Yancy, but Sadie had

said she didn't want him involved. Would she get Jordan in trouble if she brought him in on this?

She couldn't think of a better alternative, so she shuffled through the pile of papers next to the phone, found Jordan's business card and called the number. But all she got was his answering machine.

"Jordan, I know it's late. But I have a lot to tell you. Odette came here and left me a voodoo charm." She stopped, thinking how strange that must sound. She couldn't explain that whole thing to him over the phone. So she went on, "Something important happened when I picked it up, but I'll have to talk to you about it later. Sadie also called. She said she had some vital information about what happened Thursday night. She asked me to come over there. I wish you were going with me. If you get this message, maybe you can meet me." She gave him the address.

She debated about what else to say, then finally hung up. She had never been to Sadie's house, but she had the addresses of all the regulars of the Thursday-night ceremony. The older woman lived on Magnolia Drive in the exclusive neighborhood near Lake Pontchartrain.

After checking a map, she left her apartment once more. As she walked to her car, the wind was blowing and lightning crackled in the distant sky.

A storm was coming, but maybe she could beat it.

It was a twenty-minute drive to Sadie's house. On the way, she tried again to call Jordan, but he still didn't answer.

When she found the address on Magnolia Drive, she slowed. A light was burning in the front window, so she pulled into the driveway. Thunder rumbled as she climbed out of her car. If she'd been into omens, she would have taken it as a bad sign.

Around her, wind tossed the trees and bushes, and a spray of leaves came flying past her.

There were no stars visible above. Instead, a low tent of dark clouds hung over the sky, feeling as if it was pressing down on her shoulders.

Stepping under the protection of the front porch overhang, she rang the bell. Nobody answered. But when she turned the knob, the door opened and she stepped inside.

The front hall was dark, and she waited for a moment for her eyes to adjust to the dark. When they did, she saw a white-clad figure gliding toward her. Someone much too tall to be Sadie.

"Odette?"

The person didn't answer, and Camille took a quick step back, suddenly sure that coming here alone had been a big mistake.

Chapter Nine

Jordan sat in his car for a long time, debating what to do. He and Camille had made love a few days ago. It had really meant something to him. But when she'd asked her leading question, he'd climbed out of bed because all he could think was that she was going to reject him. Then she'd told him she didn't want him around her apartment—she didn't need a baby-sitter was how she'd put it. But that was after he'd clammed up and refused to talk to her.

He clenched the steering wheel. He was tired of second-guessing everything that happened between them. Tired of trying to figure out what she was thinking. He needed to talk to her. And if she told him she'd made a mistake by taking him to her bed, then he'd deal with it.

So instead of heading home, he drove to her apartment. When he got there, her car wasn't in the driveway.

He swore quietly under his breath. He was all pumped up to confront her, and she wasn't even home. Where the hell could she be after midnight on a Tuesday night?

Out with some other guy? That was the first thought

that popped into his head. He told himself it was simply his old hurt and anger surfacing. He kept seeing her through the prism of what had been, and the image was distorted. Maybe it had never been accurate.

He rang the bell—once, twice. When she didn't answer, he tried the knob, feeling his chest tighten when the door resisted his attentions.

Seized with a growing feeling of dread, he rushed back to his car and grabbed the packet of lock picks that he carried just for emergencies.

It took him only a few moments to get inside, and he figured he'd better tell her that she needed better locks.

Quickly he climbed the steps, opened the upper door and checked the apartment. It was empty. At least he hadn't found her lying on the floor or anything.

Returning to the living room, he checked the answering machine—and heard the message from Sadie Marceau.

Marceau was one of the old women from the Thursday-night voodoo club. The one that had seemed more interested in the food than the ceremony.

Had Camille gone to her house? Not a good idea, he thought. He was about to rush out the door when he halted for a moment and pressed the redial button on the phone to check the last number she'd called.

He waited impatiently while the phone rang, then felt his heart thud when he heard his own voice answer the phone.

She'd called him. He used the remote feature to get his messages—and found that she had indeed gone to Marceau's—after saying that the two of them needed to talk.

About what?

She'd mentioned a voodoo charm, and she'd said something important had happened when she'd picked it up. What the hell did she mean?

He wanted to ask her, but at the same time he wanted to wring her neck for going off alone to that old woman's house.

Cursing his own stupidity for leaving her unguarded, he charged out of the house, heading for the Lake Pontchartrain district.

With the lack of traffic on the streets, he made it to Magnolia Drive in record time. As he turned the corner, he thought he saw someone who looked like Marie Germain, Odette LaFantary's assistant. But he couldn't be sure. And he wasn't going to get off track and follow her—not when he could see Camille's car parked in Marceau's driveway.

Pulling up at the curb, he jumped out and inspected the house and grounds.

The lot was large, isolated from its neighbors by a thick screen of trees and shrubbery. The house itself was completely dark.

From the looks of the place, he would have sworn nobody was home—or they were tucked up nice and warm in bed. Only, he knew that wasn't true. At least he knew that Càmille had come here. Either she was still inside the house or somebody had taken her away.

Lightning crackled in the sky above him—as though nature had conspired to provide a backdrop for danger.

He didn't like the setup and he didn't like his choices. One was to call for backup. But he didn't know for sure that anything was wrong. All he knew was that the old lady had asked Camille to come over because she had information about the DeLyon case.

That left him where he'd started—with Detective

Yancy. He could just picture the son of a bitch waltzing in here and accusing Officer Jordan of sticking his nose where it didn't belong.

So he drew his service weapon and started up the driveway. When he reached the porch, he found the front door locked.

He could have shouted, "Police, open up."

Instead, he stood still and listened. For a moment, the wind stilled and he thought he could hear the sound of chanting and drums coming from the back yard.

Cautiously he made his way around the side of the house and came to a six-foot-tall wooden fence enclosing the back yard. But there were cracks between the slats, and through them he could see candles flickering. The small flames were accompanied by a low throbbing sound and someone chanting words he couldn't understand. But the whole deal sounded like what he'd heard on Thursday night before DeLyon had collapsed.

The hair on the back of his neck prickled as he strained his ears, listening intently. When he heard Camille, her voice slurred and frightened, he almost went crazy.

"No. Please, don't," she moaned.

"You have sealed your own fate. You must die," the other person—the one who sounded like the priestess—answered in a snarling tone.

Jordan's heart leaped into his throat. If the fence had been a couple of feet lower, he would have jumped over it into Lord knows what.

But he wasn't a superman. Desperately he looked for a quick practical way into the yard.

The spreading branches of some kind of fruit tree reached the fence. The tree was low but sturdy. Shoving his weapon back into its holster, he pulled himself up onto a low limb, then struggled to keep his balance.

The wind had picked up again, tossing the branches around, making it dangerous for him to climb higher. But he did, anyway, working toward the fence.

Carefully pushing aside the swaying branches, he looked down into the yard. As his gaze found Camille, the blood in his veins turned to ice.

She was standing in the center of the yard, facing him, stripped to the waist, her pale skin gleaming in the floodlights from the back of the house. Her head lolled to one side, and her arms were stretched out.

What he was seeing was so bizarre that it took a moment to realize that her wrists were tied to the two sturdy posts of a garden arbor.

Drums pounded in the background. Where were the drummers? The only person he saw with Camille was a figure wearing white robes and a white headdress.

"What…what did I do?" Camille asked, sounding scared and groggy. She was obviously fighting to bring her head upright. "Please tell me. I have a right to know."

"You have no right. No rights at all. You must pay."

The priestess turned away from Camille, and Jordan saw that the figure was wearing a mask that completely covered her face. He didn't really know whether it was a man or a woman under that getup. But he kept thinking of her as the priestess because she was dressed like the woman he'd seen at the restaurant.

From up in the tree, he didn't have a clear shot at the figure, especially when he wasn't even standing on solid ground. Especially when the person was so close to Camille.

He wanted to spring out of the tree into the yard, but

what if the drummers he heard came charging out and overpowered him?

He saw the priestess bend to a wicker basket sitting on a low table, then quickly open the lid and reach inside. As he watched her careful movements, his brain struggled to process what he was seeing.

It looked as if she was holding up a wriggling stick, grasping it near one end and in the middle. But then he realized that the writhing, wiggling rod was a snake.

And not just any snake. A rattlesnake.

He recognized the markings from a recent training course the department had suggested he take. At the time, he'd resented the extra hours. Now he was damn glad he'd done it.

Before he could react, the priestess thrust the viper toward Camille's breast. She screamed and cringed back. For a terrible moment, he thought the poisonous fangs had pierced her flesh. Then he realized that it was just a taunting pass from the priestess.

But the next attack might well be for real.

With no thought for his own safety, he leaped out of the tree, aiming for the white-clad figure and knocking the snake out of her hand. Off balance, he came down heavily on his butt.

He was trying to push himself up when something soft and dry slithered over his hand.

The rattlesnake! Whipping his head around, he saw it slither away into the bushes.

He was just breathing out a sigh of relief when a movement on his left caught his eye, and he swung around to face the priestess. She had scrambled away from him and picked up a small metal statue. When she swung it viciously at him, he ducked.

He took a glancing blow to the side of the face. Then a foot lashed out at him, catching him in the knee.

While he was on the ground, his attacker turned and charged into the house.

He pushed himself up and followed. Dashing through the interior, he found the front door wide open. The woman had escaped into the night. And there was no sign of anyone else in the house or in the yard.

He wanted to go after the priestess and haul her back. But he had to keep his priorities straight. The snake was still in the yard with Camille.

Turning, he ran back the way he'd come.

The rattler had disappeared, but the drums were still booming in the darkness.

Half expecting someone to leap out of the bushes and assault him, he ran to Camille, who was on her feet, her hands still secured to the arbor posts. But now she was slumped to the side, moaning.

"I'm here," he called to her. Halfway across the patio, he almost tripped over a tape recorder lying on the ground. When he realized the background drums were coming from the machine, he cursed and picked the damn thing up, smashing it against the concrete.

Hearing the sound, Camille raised her head in his direction, but he could tell she was having trouble focusing on him.

"It's Jordan. Everything's okay."

"Odette…?"

"She got away. The cops will scoop her up," he said, hoping it was true.

While he spoke, he worked at the rope that secured her right wrist to a post. As soon as he'd untied one hand, he gathered her to him, holding her body protectively.

She felt so cold and limp in his arms that he wanted to scream. Instead, he clamped his teeth together and worked as quickly as he could, feeling the wind whipping at them.

Finally he freed her, and she collapsed against him just as rain began to spatter the yard. Lifting her up and cradling her in his arms, he strode quickly inside. After kicking the door shut, he looked around the family room. There was a plump sofa against the wall, and he crossed to it, lowering himself to a seated position while he held her close and stroked her back and shoulders.

"Camille, are you all right? What did she do to you?"

"I'm okay…now. She…shoved something over my head. I…I couldn't breathe. I don't remember much after that." She raised her face and looked through the window at the yard, where rain now pelted the ground. Blinking, she whispered, "I guess she dragged me outside and tied me up."

When he shifted her in his arms, she gripped his shoulders. "Don't let me go," she begged. "Just get me out of this place. I want to go home."

He smoothed his hand over her hair. "I will. But I can't do it yet. I need to call this in. And first I need to cover you up."

Her gaze dropped to her bare arms, then her chest. "My blouse is gone," she said in a confused voice. "You can see my breasts."

He swallowed. "Yeah." Slipping off his jacket, he helped her get her arms through the sleeves, then worked the zipper so that her torso was covered.

After he'd made the call, he turned back to her. "I listened to the message on your answering machine. Do you think Sadie was working with the priestess?'' he asked. ''Did Odette use Sadie to lure you over here?''

''I don't know,'' she answered, her speech still slurred. ''Why would Odette have needed help? I would have come if she had called me.''

He had no answer for that, but he had another question of his own. ''Did you see Sadie when you arrived?''

Her brow wrinkled. ''No.''

So had the old lady split? Or had the voodoo priestess bagged her?

While he was still puzzling over the details, two uniformed officers arrived.

One was Billy Ward, a guy who'd been at the Police Academy with him. The other was Zachary Doucet.

He groaned inwardly, wishing his half brother hadn't caught the call. But apparently Zach could see the tension radiating off Jordan, because he played it very cool, staring at him out of his heavy-lidded green eyes that were so unnervingly like their father's.

Together Jordan, Zach and Billy made a quick search of the house. It appeared there'd been a struggle in the den. A chair was overturned and some knickknacks had been knocked to the floor. But there was no sign of Sadie.

Next he and Camille both gave an account of what had happened, and Jordan was glad that she sounded more coherent as the interview went on, which told him that the effects of whatever Odette had given her were wearing off.

Still, she looked exhausted by the time they'd finished.

''She's had a pretty rough time and she needs to get

out of here,'' he said. ''She'll be available for more extensive questioning later.''

''Take all the time you need,'' Zach said, the sincerity of his voice startling Jordan.

''Thanks,'' he managed to say. ''Then I'll take her home.''

When he guided her through the rain to the car, she sat down heavily in the passenger seat.

Asking her to wait, he went back and gave the two other cops the address and phone number.

Zach raised an eyebrow when he heard the information, but didn't say anything.

When Jordan returned to the car, Camille was sitting with her eyes closed. By the time he backed up and started down the street, she was sleeping.

She awoke when the car stopped again. Sitting up, she looked around in confusion.

''Where are we?''

''At my place.''

''But—''

''No arguments. As long as Odette is on the loose, I'm going to keep you safe. And I can do it better here than at your place.''

He was glad that the living room of his little house was reasonably neat and that he'd made the bed before leaving that morning. Quickly he pulled aside the covers. When he turned back to her, she was struggling out of his jacket.

In the morning she might regret stripping to the waist. For now she seemed too out of it to notice.

Getting in bed with her was turning into a habit, he thought as he pulled off everything but his underwear and joined her under the covers.

WEAK MORNING SUNLIGHT was filtering through the window when Jordan awoke to find Camille lying on her side, facing him, the covers pulled over the tops of her breasts.

"How are you?" he asked.

"Better than I was last night, thanks to you. Did I dream it, or did Odette come at me with a snake?"

He swallowed. "You didn't dream it."

"You saved my life, didn't you?"

He nodded.

"You could have gotten bitten, instead of me. You were taking a big chance."

He nodded again, then decided to level with her, because as far as he was concerned, he had nothing left to lose. Still, his heart was pounding when he said, "Camille, you might not want to hear this, but I care about you."

"I do want to hear it!"

"You do?"

"Yes. But first I have to explain something." She gave him a perplexed look. "If the cops come up with evidence against Odette, I'll accept that she did it. But I don't understand why she would want to hurt me, because before I went to Sadie's house, Odette came to me with a voodoo charm."

His hands tightened on her arms. "Bad medicine? More gris-gris?"

"No, good medicine! A pretty little silk bag with beads sewn onto it. She said it was something I needed. After she left, when I held it in my hand, I saw the past. I saw my mom destroying a letter at the mailbox. So I went home and confronted her." Tears thickened her voice as she went on, "She admitted that she'd stolen the letters you wrote me when you were at your uncle's.

She told me that she made your mother cooperate with her because she wanted each of us to think that the other wasn't writing. She did that to us, and I'm so ashamed of her.''

"They did that to us? Your mother and mine?'' he asked, hardly able to wrap his mind around it.

"It was my mother's idea. Yours didn't have any choice if she wanted to keep her job.''

He couldn't hold back a curse.

"Oh, Jordan, I'm so sorry. As soon as I found out, I wanted to call you. And then I got the message from Sadie. And thank God you came over there and found me. I guess you got my message.''

He couldn't hide his embarrassed expression. "Not until after I'd unlocked your door and listened to your answering machine.''

"So you were worried about me,'' she said, sliding toward him, reaching for him.

"Yeah, I was,'' he answered, hauling her close.

"Jordan, as soon as I saw you at the restaurant, I knew my feelings for you hadn't changed. But every time I tried to talk to you…''

"I was too afraid to listen,'' he finished for her.

"Afraid?''

"That you were going to rip my heart out again. So I kept running away before you could hurt me.''

"Oh, no. Oh, Jordan. Never.''

She raised her face, finding his lips with hers, the kiss going from comforting to passionate in the space of a heartbeat.

He kissed her with the same fervor, his blood heating as he absorbed what she'd told him and absorbed the reality of her in his arms, in his bed.

She drew back, just enough to speak against his lips.

"We wasted so much time. I don't want to waste another minute."

"No."

He kissed her mouth, her eyelids, her jaw, as his hands shifted to cup her breasts.

She made a low greedy sound as he caressed her, found her hardened nipples with his fingers and played with them.

"I love that," she murmured. "I love *you*."

He raised his head, looking down at her. "I thought I'd never hear you say that."

Her eyes shone into his. "I have. For a long time. Only, I was so sad that you'd turned away from me."

He shook his head. "Camille, I've loved you since I was a kid. You were the princess in the fairy tale and I was the commoner who didn't have a chance with you."

"You always had my heart."

"I thought you'd decided you were ashamed of the things we'd done together."

"Never. You were the one who taught me passion."

"I think we taught each other."

"Uh-huh. But am I going to be the one who asks where this is leading now?"

He swallowed hard, still half-afraid that the dream would slip away. Yet he was able to say, "I told that old guy, Mr. Fitch, I was your fiancé. I think I said it because of how much I wanted it to be true. Even if I couldn't admit it. So, will you marry me?"

"Oh, yes."

"A big successful restaurant owner can have a cop for a husband?"

"You think I'm big?" she teased.

"You know what I mean."

"Yes, well, to make my position perfectly clear, this restaurant owner can do anything she wants in her personal life. And I do want to be married to a cop—as long as his name is Jordan O'Reilly."

Before he could ask any more questions, she lowered her mouth to his again, cutting off the conversation, bringing them back to where they'd left off.

And this time their lovemaking was all the sweeter, because they both knew they were making a commitment, not just giving each other pleasure. A commitment to moving on into a long loving future together. The future they had both so desperately wanted but had been afraid would never be theirs.

LIAM

ANN VOSS PETERSON

Chapter One

Heart hammering, Liam O'Reilly slammed the squad car's door and raced to the front door of Jordan's bungalow. He had to talk to his baby brother. He had to talk to him *now*. And he couldn't break news like this over the phone.

Reaching the door, he beat on it with a fist. Rustling and the low hum of voices reached Liam's ears.

Finally the door opened a crack, and one of Jordan's green eyes peered out. "Liam? What the hell's wrong?" Jordan yanked open the door. Naked to the waist, he held his Sig in one hand, barrel pointed at the floor.

"Who's here?" Camille emerged from the bedroom wrapped in one of Jordan's bathrobes, bare feet apart as if she was ready to take on the world.

Liam stepped into the room and closed the door behind him. He nodded in the direction of the bedroom. "You'd better get dressed. Both of you."

Jordan grabbed his shirt from the back of a chair and shrugged into it. "What happened?"

"It's Yancy. He's looking for you."

"Why so urgent?" He glanced at a clock on the wall.

"We filled out a report last night. Can't his questions wait until after breakfast, for God's sake?"

"He got the tox screen back on DeLyon."

"What did he find?"

"Poison."

Jordan's lips straightened into a bloodless line. "So he *was* murdered."

Liam nodded. "They found a derivative of tetradotoxin. A derivative that's very deadly and acts quickly in the bloodstream. A pinprick and DeLyon was dead in minutes."

Camille raised wide eyes to Jordan. "What's tetradotoxin?"

"Pufferfish toxin. Legend has it voodoo practitioners use it to turn people into zombies."

"Voodoo? Then that points to Odette, too." She shook her head as if she couldn't believe it.

"Not exactly," Liam said. "Yancy's under the impression it points to Jordan."

Jordan swore. "I ran into it on a bust a few months ago. It was the type of derivative Liam was talking about." He looked to Liam for verification.

Liam nodded. "Yancy searched your locker at the station this morning. I heard through the grapevine he's claiming he found tetradotoxin."

"That son of a bitch. Yancy planted it. He had to."

Liam nodded. As soon as he'd heard, he'd known the tetradotoxin had been planted. "Word is that Yancy has an arrest warrant for you."

"No." Camille stepped back as if the news hit her with the force of a physical blow. "Jordan didn't kill anyone."

Liam held up a hand. "That's not all. They found Sadie Marceau's body."

"Oh, God, Sadie?" Camille swayed on unsteady feet. "I was afraid something terrible had happened to her."

Jordan wrapped an arm around her and pulled her close. "Where did they find her?"

"At her house. In the gardening shed. Her throat was slashed." He paused, trying to work up the courage to force the words from his lips. "You were there last night."

"Odette—" Jordan glanced at Camille "—or, at least, someone dressed as a voodoo priestess lured Camille over there. She tried to kill Camille with a poisonous snake."

Camille clutched Jordan's hand. She raised her chin determinedly, as if finding a source of inner strength. "Sadie called me. She said she knew something about Spiro DeLyon's death. She wanted me to come to her house. But when I arrived, she wasn't there." Camille stopped, choking back a sob.

Liam nodded. He'd heard about the events of the night before. The events surrounding Sadie Marceau's death. "And now Yancy has it in his damn-fool head that Jordan killed Sadie, too."

Blood crept up Jordan's neck.

Liam laid a hand on his brother's arm. Jordan might have the O'Reilly temper, but he didn't kill DeLyon or Sadie Marceau. Liam would stake his life on it. "We have to figure out what we're going to do."

Camille turned to Jordan, her eyes frantically searching his. "You have to get out of here, Jordan. You can hide until we can prove you didn't do it."

"I'm an officer of the law. It'll be better if I turn myself in."

Liam blew out a relieved breath. He knew Jordan would choose to do the right thing. The only prudent thing under the circumstances. "I'll drive you to the station."

Tears sparkled in Camille's eyes. "They'll put you in jail. We just found each other again. I can't lose you now."

Jordan gathered her into his arms. "You aren't going to lose me. No one will come between us ever again. I promise."

Brushing tears away with the back of her hand, Camille nodded. "I love you, Jordan."

"I love you, too, Camille. More than I can say."

Liam crossed the room to the window to give them a moment of privacy. Jordan had finally claimed the woman who'd stolen his heart when they were only children. At least one of the O'Reilly brothers would marry. At least one would carry on the family name. Provided he could get Jordan out of this mess.

An unmarked Crown Victoria swung onto the street followed by two squad cars. They stopped behind Liam's cruiser. Liam's gut tightened. "It's too late. Yancy's here."

Jordan barely had time to pull on his shoes before the knock on the door reverberated through the room. "Police. Open up."

Liam strode to the door and pulled it open.

Decked out in his usual tailored suit and silk tie, Yancy scowled up at him. "Why are you here, Liam? Trying to warn little brother? Give him a chance to run?"

Liam gritted his teeth. He'd never liked Yancy. The man was a bantam rooster looking for a fight. And a promotion. He always acted as if he had some kind of beef with the O'Reillys. "I'm here to drive Jordan to the station. He was about to turn himself in."

"Right. And I'm Emeril Lagasse." Yancy pushed his way into the room. Long dark hair secured in a braid, Yancy's partner, Rebecca Romero, stepped in behind him. Two uniforms followed. Yancy surveyed the room and grunted low in his throat. "I'll be mentioning this to your supervisor, Liam, you can bet on that. You'll be lucky to walk away with a suspension."

Liam balled his hands into fists at his sides. The last thing he needed was to be suspended while Yancy built a case against Jordan. He would be cut out of the loop just when being in the loop could do Jordan the most good.

Judging from the smug grin on Yancy's face, the bastard knew exactly what he was doing. And he was enjoying it far too much. "There's nothing more disgusting than a dirty cop. Except maybe a family of dirty cops." Yancy glanced over his shoulder. "Romero? You want to do the honors? I'm afraid if I try to cuff this son of a bitch, I might do something to break your precious rules. Or his precious face."

Romero shot Liam an apologetic look before focusing on Jordan. She pulled a pair of cuffs from under the jacket of her pantsuit. "Put your hands behind your back, Jordan."

Jordan turned around and did as she instructed.

She snapped the cuffs on his wrists and started reciting his Miranda rights.

Behind Jordan, Camille grasped the back of a chair.

Liam stepped to her side. "Jordan is going to need a lawyer, Camille. A good one. Can you find him one?"

She set her quivering chin and nodded, as if grateful to have something, anything, to do. "I know someone."

"Good. Have him meet us at the station right away. And, Camille?"

She focused teary eyes on him.

''Try your best not to worry. I'll clear Jordan. I won't let my brother be locked away for a crime he didn't commit. I promise you that.''

Chapter Two

Liam paced the hall outside the interrogation room where Jordan was being held. As soon as he'd reached the station, he'd been called to the carpet by his supervisor. And as a result, for the first time in his career, Liam was suspended while his supervisor investigated Yancy's accusation that he was helping Jordan escape arrest.

No gun. No badge. No uniform. The news had swept through the station with the speed of hurricane winds. Now nobody on the force would talk to him, let alone shuttle any information about Jordan's case his way.

Liam clenched his hands into fists. He wanted to slam one into the wall. Or into Yancy's face. He hated being so powerless. It was a pain he hadn't felt since he was seventeen. A pain he never wanted to feel again.

He forced himself to lean against the wall, crossing his ankles. The cumbersome weight of his ankle holster rubbed against his opposite leg. He may have lost his service pistol, along with his badge, but at least he still had the backup .22 he always carried. So he wasn't totally powerless.

''I'm here to see Jordan O'Reilly,'' an in-charge feminine voice announced.

Liam's head jerked up. Striding toward him, blond corkscrew curls framing her pretty face, lush red lips tensed into a battle line, was none other than Simone Jones.

His gut tightened. His pulse picked up its pace. He'd faced the defense attorney in court several times. Of course he'd only needed to experience her brand of cross-examination once to know all he needed to know about her. She might look as cute as Meg Ryan in one of those quirky comedies, but she was as ruthless as a shark that smelled blood in the water.

He stepped in front of her, barring her path. "What do you want with Jordan?"

The fluorescent lights reflected off a large Pegasus brooch pinned over one breast of her power suit. She stopped a few inches from him, a golden wing nearly touching his chest, and looked up. Slightly tilted at the outside corners, her blue eyes were as exotic as her scent. "Hello, Officer O'Reilly."

He pushed away from the wall and uncrossed his ankles, positioning one foot slightly behind the other for balance. "What do you want with Jordan?" he repeated.

"I've been retained to represent him. Your brother is my client."

Liam took a step back. If he'd been thinking straight, he wouldn't have been surprised. There was no other reason for her to be at the station this morning asking to see Jordan. But somehow she'd caught him off guard. She always did. And that was the thing about her that drove him craziest. "Camille DuPree called you?"

Her lips softened. "Camille's a friend of mine. A good friend. I'd move heaven and earth to help her and her fiancé. Your brother is in good hands, Liam."

He wanted to believe her, for Jordan's sake. And everything he knew about Simone suggested she could defend Jordan against any charge the DA could throw at him. But Liam had learned long ago not to trust anything he couldn't control. And he didn't have the slightest idea how to control Simone Jones.

Across the hall, he spotted Yancy. A thick folder under one arm, the detective started in the direction of the interrogation room where Jordan was being held.

Simone followed Liam's gaze. Raising a hand, she raced across the hall. "You're not on your way to question my client without his counsel present, are you, Detective?"

Yancy turned in Simone's direction. "So you're defending O'Reilly. Now why doesn't that make my day?"

Clearly the detective wasn't happy to see her. A fact that warmed Liam's own feelings toward her. At least a little.

Simone smiled. "You know the law, Detective. I'd hate to make trouble for you by accusing you of not following it. Now if you don't mind, I'd like to speak with my client alone."

"Take all the time you want. He ain't going anywhere but death row."

"We'll see about that." Without a glance over her shoulder, Simone breezed into the interrogation room.

Liam watched her go. Despite his unease around Simone Jones, he had to admit she was an impressive woman. Maybe it was a good thing she was on Jordan's side. A smart and aggressive attorney was exactly what Jordan needed. That and some exculpatory evidence.

And suspension or not, that was where Liam could help.

He leaned back against the wall. Watching the closed door, he waited for Simone to emerge from the interrogation room. When she did twenty minutes later, he stepped into her path. "I need a word with you."

She glanced down at her watch. "Then walk with me. I have to make a stop before my next appointment at eleven."

He fell in beside her. As soon as he stepped outside, heat and humidity hit him like a wall. Rainwater pooled in the cracks and dips of cobblestone, the only evidence of last night's storm.

She glanced at Liam and slipped on a pair of sunglasses. "So what's this word you wanted with me?"

"I want Jordan to have the best defense he can get. So I'm going to help."

She stared at him for a moment, as if mulling over the proposal. "I appreciate the offer, Liam. I really do. But I have an investigator who does my legwork for me."

"He's not as motivated as I am. And I bet he doesn't work free. I do."

"This doesn't have anything to do with the fact that you don't trust me, does it?"

"You're good at your job. I know that."

"That's not what I said. You don't trust me. Why?"

"No cop trusts defense attorneys."

"But your distrust is personal."

What could he say? That every time he was near her, he felt off balance? That his gut tensed? That his heart raced? He'd sound like one of those pathetic men who was afraid of strong women. Or worse, a schoolboy with a crush. "I've been suspended. The only way I can help my brother is by helping you."

"Suspended? Why?"

He told her about Yancy's assertion that he was trying to help Jordan escape arrest.

"And were you?" She raised her eyebrows in question.

"I was planning to take him to the station to turn himself in." He held his hands out, palms up. "Jordan didn't kill anyone. You have to let me help you prove it."

She pressed her lips into a thoughtful line. Finally she nodded. "You've got the job." She held out her hand and smiled, her nose crinkling like a girl's. "Welcome aboard."

He grasped her hand and shook. Her grip was firm, her skin impossibly soft. A frisson of heat traveled through him, making his head feel light. The tension in his gut racheted up another notch. He'd gotten exactly what he wanted. A role in Jordan's defense. A chance to do something to help his brother. He should be happy.

Why, then, did he feel more out of control than ever?

SIMONE LISTENED to the steady footfalls of Officer Liam O'Reilly as he walked beside her down Conti Street. Although well-worn jeans encased his thighs and a New Orleans Saints T-shirt stretched across his broad chest rather than a blue uniform, he still looked every inch the cop. From his squared-off haircut to his always-ready posture, Liam didn't have to wear the blue to be in uniform. He *was* the uniform. And more gorgeous than any movie cop who'd graced the silver screen.

She pulled her gaze away and concentrated on the uneven cobblestones under her feet. She must have lost her mind, agreeing to work with him. If Liam O'Reilly was anything, it was strong-willed. Cross-examining him in court had always been a battle. And no doubt working with him on his brother's case would be even more challenging.

Of course, like any litigator, she loved a good fight.

Reaching Chartres Street, Simone turned left, heading deeper into the French Quarter.

Liam hesitated. "I thought your office was in the CBD."

She nodded, surprised he knew her office was in the central business district. "I have to make a stop, remember?"

Falling back into step with her, he eyed her, one brow raised as though waiting for an explanation.

She sighed. "Every time I get a big case, I stop at a friend's shop."

"A friend?"

"A voodoo priestess. She makes a special gris-gris for me. Since I started carrying one into court, I haven't lost a case."

"I've heard of cops carrying gris-gris to protect them on the streets." His brows dipped. "Do you really believe in that stuff?"

His doubt didn't surprise her. She'd be willing to bet Liam O'Reilly didn't believe in anything he couldn't document in a police report. Of course, if she was honest, she'd have to admit she wasn't sure about voodoo herself. "To tell you the truth, I'm still searching for something to believe in."

A scoff slipped from his lips.

She tried not to smile. "What do you believe in?"

"Not myths and superstitious nonsense, that's for sure. I have control over my own life."

"Well, I'm glad you're so sure of yourself. I like to hedge my bets. Besides, I figure even if you don't believe in voodoo, you might be interested in accompanying me.''

''How's that?''

''The voodoo priestess who makes the gris-gris for me is Odette LaFantary.''

Liam's eyes brightened. ''You're right. I would be interested. Very interested.''

''I'm glad we agree on something.''

LIAM GLANCED AROUND at the slick peach-and-silver interior in the front room of Odette's shop. He'd never been inside a voodoo shop, but this light modern decor was far from what his imagination had conjured up on the walk over. He glanced at Simone. ''You're sure this is the right place?''

She nodded, her blond curls bobbing with the movement. ''She sells natural cosmetics. The voodoo is in the back.'' Motioning to him, she crossed the shop, her heels clicking on gray tile. She slipped into the adjoining room.

Liam followed. As soon as his eyes adjusted to the dim light, he saw the red and gold colors, and the skulls, dolls, feathers and candles he expected. A regal-looking African-American woman turned from one of the displays. Her face wore a reserved smile. ''Simone. I knew you would be coming. I saw it in the cards this morning.'' Her voice was deep and touched with a hint of Haiti.

''Then you know why I'm here. Jordan O'Reilly has been arrested for Spiro DeLyon's murder.''

''Yes. I'm nearly finished making the gris-gris. A powerful gris-gris to protect an innocent man.'' Her gaze shifted to Liam. She said nothing, just watched him with hooded eyes.

"Odette, this is Liam O'Reilly, Jordan's brother."

The voodoo priestess nodded. "I saw his coming in the cards, also."

Liam shifted uncomfortably. All this darkness and voodoo and talk of seeing the future in cards was getting to him. Now he even had the feeling he was being watched. "I have a few questions for you, Ms. La-Fantary."

"I doubt I have the answers you want. The spirits have shown me little about your brother's fate."

Liam shook his head. "Those aren't the answers I'm after. I'm more interested in the past than in some mystical future. I want to know where you were last night."

A bell tinkled. Odette glanced at an open door in the back of the room. "Marie? We have a customer."

A slender girl with skin the color of café au lait appeared in the doorway. She crossed the room and stepped into the cosmetics shop. Liam spotted an older woman standing among the silver and peach.

"Mrs. Guidry. She is a good customer. If you'll excuse me..." Odette grasped something from the counter behind her and went out into the cosmetics shop. The hum of friendly greetings filtered into the back room.

Simone glanced in the direction of the sound and frowned at Liam. "You want to know where Odette was last night? You don't really think she attacked Camille, do you?"

"Why wouldn't I?"

"Because she wouldn't do something like that. Not to Camille. Not to anyone."

"And you base this on what?"

"I know her."

"Not a good defense, Counselor. You should know that."

"Maybe not, but I know what I know. Odette wouldn't hurt anyone."

"Glad you're so sure. I'll leave my judgments until I see the evidence."

Odette glided back into the voodoo portion of the shop. "Now I will answer your questions. If I can."

"Where were you last night?" Liam repeated.

"I was here working on the gris-gris I just delivered to Mrs. Guidry. And some other spells."

"What kind of other spells?"

Odette glanced at Simone before returning her gaze to Liam. "Nothing you need to know about."

"Trust me, I need to know."

Odette stepped to the counter and counted out nine sprigs of some type of herb. She slipped the herbs into a small pouch already filled with other herbs and God knows what. With deft fingers, she closed the pouch and tied it with a piece of beaded lace. She looked up at Liam, her dark eyes meeting his gaze. "I didn't kill Sadie Marceau, if that is what you want to know."

"How did you know about Sadie's death? It won't hit the *Times-Picayune* until tomorrow."

Odette pressed her lips into a flat line and said nothing.

She didn't have to. He knew what her answer would be. "I suppose the spirits revealed Sadie Marceau's murder to you in the cards, too."

"Not until after it happened."

"And DeLyon? Did the spirits tell you he was going to be poisoned?"

"I don't see everything. Only what the spirits reveal."

"Convenient. And you expect me to believe all this?"

"I tell the truth, Liam O'Reilly. It's up to you to believe or not to believe."

Liam took a deep breath. The last thing he wanted was to get in a discussion about beliefs. He needed facts, not superstition. "Sadie was a regular attendee of the Thursday-night voodoo ceremonies at Camille DuPree's restaurant, Chez Camille, wasn't she?"

"She never missed a ceremony."

"And neither did Spiro DeLyon."

She gave a single nod.

"And now they're both dead."

Odette's face hardened, the dim light reflecting off her high cheekbones.

Simone tilted her head. "Who else regularly attended the ceremonies, Odette?"

The priestess turned to Simone, her face softening slightly. "Miss Lulu DeLyon, of course. A friend of the DeLyons, Tony Fortune. Sadie's sister, Helen." The bell tinkled again, cutting off her recitation. She looked in the direction of the cosmetics shop.

Voices reached into the back room. The soft voice of Odette's assistant, Marie, followed by a sharp frightened-sounding voice.

Odette crossed to the doorway. "Lisa, what is the problem?"

A young woman rushed up to her, a paper bag clutched in one hand. "Oh, my God. That was Mrs. Guidry who just left the shop, wasn't it?"

Odette laid a calming hand on the young woman's arm. "Yes."

"But she's *walking*."

"I asked the *loa* for her healing. They answered."

Lisa shook her head, her straight brown hair lashing against her cheeks. "She was in a wheelchair. You can't just ask the gods to heal her one moment and have her walking the next.''

"The *loa* can do many things. Isn't that why you joined the group, Lisa? Didn't you believe the spirits could reverse your bad fortune?''

"I don't know. I hoped, but—''

"What is in the bag, child?''

"I...'' Lisa looked down at her hand as if she'd forgotten she held the paper bag. Her eyes widened with a fresh flash of fear. "I found it on my doorstep.''

Odette took the bag. She crossed to the counter where Simone and Liam stood and dumped out the contents.

A misshapen black lump bristling with feathers fell onto the counter.

A gasp sounded from the other side of the room.

Liam turned toward the sound.

Odette's assistant, Marie, stood in the doorway. "Another evil charm,'' she breathed. "That other couple brought one in. The chef and the cop.''

Liam nodded. Jordan had told him about the voodoo charm Camille had received. A charm that sounded a lot like the one on the counter now.

Odette narrowed her eyes at the lump. "I don't like this.''

Lisa looked at her. "What does it mean?''

"It means you are in danger.'' She turned to Liam. "This is Lisa Cantro. She is another regular member of the Thursday-night group.''

Lisa's eyes were still glued to Odette. "Danger? What kind of danger?''

"That, I don't know. But you must go home, lock your doors and don't let anyone inside. Not even someone you know and trust. I will try to do something about this.''

The young woman nodded. Without another word, she whirled and headed out the door of the shop.

Simone leaned over the counter, studying the lump. "Who would make such a thing?"

"Someone with murder in his heart." Odette's voice was flat, unemotional, and Liam got the idea she hadn't been surprised by the evil charm. Not surprised at all.

"Have you made charms like this one?" he asked.

The priestess held up a hand. "I won't answer any more questions. I have my work to do. You have yours. Let's hope that between the two of us, we can stop this evil from taking another life." She handed the velvet pouch she'd been working on earlier to Simone, then with two strides, swept through the doorway at the back of the shop and disappeared. Marie filed out in her wake.

Chapter Three

Simone stopped in front of the building that housed her office suite and eyed Liam. He'd been looking over his shoulder the entire walk from Odette's shop in the French Quarter to Simone's office on the edge of the CBD. Something was definitely bothering him. Something beyond the fact that Odette had refused to answer more questions. "What is it?"

He shot her a look as if he didn't know what she was talking about.

"Something is bothering you."

"Did the *loa* tell you that? Or did you get it from that voodoo gris-gris?"

"Don't be a smart-ass. I figured it out because your head's been on a swivel since we left Odette's."

He let out a sigh, as if deciding it was time to come clean. "I can't shake the feeling that someone's watching us."

"Odette said there's evil around. Don't tell me you're starting to believe."

He looked at her out of the corner of his eye and gave a perfunctory laugh. "Whatever the source, I do believe there's danger. You need to be careful."

"Whoever's responsible isn't after me."

"You don't know that. Someone's killing people and trying to focus the blame on my brother. You're defending him. It's possible you'll become a target."

Warmth seeped through her at his concerned tone. She tossed him a teasing smile. "If I didn't know better, I'd say you were worried about me. Quite a change from your usual antagonism."

Liam seemed unsure how to respond.

Simone couldn't help but chuckle. Liam definitely disliked being off balance. Which only made her want to shake him up more. Still, it had been a long time since someone had been worried about her safety. It was nice to know he was concerned. More than nice. "I have a late night, but I'll take a cab directly to my door after work."

He frowned, his brows lowering over those sexy penetrating green eyes.

She shifted her briefcase and the gris-gris she'd gotten from Odette to her left hand, then raised her right as if swearing to tell nothing but the truth, so help her God. "I'll be careful. I promise."

He paused for a moment, then nodded. "I'll do some digging into the regulars at Odette's voodoo ceremonies. Call me on my cell phone when you get home. I'll let you know what I find." Giving her his card with one hand, he held the building's door open with the other.

Once she stepped inside, he turned and walked back down the street. But even as she watched him stride off, she couldn't help thinking about how warm his concern for her made her feel. And how much she looked forward to talking to him tonight.

THE LONG DAY of hearings and evening of depositions and paperwork had worn on Simone, and she was bone tired by the time she collapsed into the cab for the six block jaunt to her house on Dauphine Street. But despite her fatigue, a sense of unease trilled along her nerves.

Damn Liam and his warnings. She'd never felt afraid going home at night before. She'd have to tell him to keep his paranoia to himself when she called him.

Reaching the little house with its quaint courtyard garden she'd bought last year, she paid the cabbie, gave him a generous tip to wait until she got inside the gate, and climbed out of the cab into the humid June night. She fitted her key into the elaborate wrought-iron gate that led to the front door and back to the courtyard. The gate swung open easily under her hand. She turned and waved to the cabbie before letting herself inside. After locking the gate behind her, she walked down the side corridor to the door of her house. She was just cursing Liam's paranoia again under her breath when she spotted something dark next to the potted kalanchoe on her doorstep. "What in the world?" She bent down to study the object.

The dim illumination from the converted gas lamps lighting the courtyard reflected off the slick black surface. Black feathers stuck to the side of the lump, just like the voodoo charm Lisa Cantro had brought to Odette this morning. She was so focused on the charm it took a few seconds to realize she heard a sound. Footsteps...

An arm clamped down on her throat before she could straighten. Hard as steel, it cut off her scream.

Chapter Four

A strangled scream ripped down the narrow street.

Adrenaline surged into Liam's bloodstream. He jammed on the brakes, slammed his car into park and threw open the door. He was running before his feet hit the pavement. Someone was in trouble. And he knew in his gut it was Simone.

He pulled the .22 from his ankle holster and raced to the gate enclosing the courtyard. Grabbing the wrought iron, he pushed. The lock held fast.

Damn.

A space gaped between the top of the gate and the stone wall. But while a woman or small man might be able to fit through the gap, there wasn't a chance he could.

He squinted, trying to see through the shadows. Two figures were struggling near the entry to the courtyard. Two women, if he wasn't mistaken. And judging from the glint of blond hair in the dim light, one was Simone.

He raised his gun, but didn't press the trigger. He didn't dare shoot. He could hit Simone as easily as her attacker. "Police! On your knees and put your hands behind your head!"

Tangled together, the shadows froze. Then one leg flashed back in a kick.

A pained grunt echoed off the surrounding brick walls. One dark shape stumbled backward.

Simone kicked again.

The attacker lurched forward, regaining her hold on Simone's throat.

Liam yanked and pushed on the gate. Dread throbbed in his chest. He had to get inside. He had to help Simone. He stepped back and leveled the barrel of his weapon on the ancient iron lock. Praying the bullet wouldn't ricochet, he squeezed the trigger.

The shot split the air, the narrow corridor amplifying the report.

The dark figure released Simone's throat.

Simone fell to her knees, gasping for breath.

Liam grabbed the gate and pushed. The lock held. When he threw his body against the wrought iron, it gave a protesting groan. One more push and the gate swung open.

Liam leveled his gun, ready to shoot. "Facedown on the ground! Do it now!"

The attacker twisted around. But instead of dropping to the cobblestone, she dodged around the corner of the house and into the courtyard.

Liam raced down the corridor to Simone.

Coughing, Simone waved him on. "I'm okay. Go."

Relief flooded Liam in a wave. He continued running down the corridor and into the courtyard.

The enclosed space was small but lush with plants. Dark wrought-iron furniture hulked in the center, flanked by magnolia, elephant ears and the long leaves of banana. Water trickled from the mouth of a bacchanalian face and splashed into a pool surrounded by moss-covered brick and ferns. Above the sound of the fountain, Liam caught the scuff of a shoe against stone.

The wall. Whoever had attacked Simone must have climbed the English ivy and slipped over the brick into the neighboring courtyard.

He moved closer to the fountain, ears straining to catch another sound. But only the trickle of water broke the stillness.

"WHOEVER SHE WAS, she's long gone." Liam stepped past Simone into the small entry hall of her house. After making sure she was safely inside, he'd called the police. The responding officers had spent the past two hours questioning Simone and him and scouring the area. They'd found nothing.

Simone closed the door and slid the dead bolt home. Turning, she tilted her head back and looked up at him. "You saved my life tonight."

Her clear blue eyes sparkled in the dim entry hall. Her pale face looked so…so vulnerable. Before tonight he never would have used that word to describe Simone Jones. But as he looked into her eyes, that was the word that came to mind.

Vulnerable…fragile…sweet.

He shook his head, trying to erase the path his mind was traveling. Ever since he'd met Simone, she'd gotten under his skin. First in the courtroom, and now. "It was nothing. If I hadn't been there, you would have gotten away on your own."

"I'm glad I didn't have to." She reached out and lay her fingers on his arm. "Thank you."

A hint of warmth shimmered over his skin at her touch. A hint of warmth that made him hunger for more.

He should turn and continue down the hall to the

living room. He should put some distance between them. But his feet wouldn't move. The urge to take her into his arms, to feel her heart beating against his chest, to let her know how frightened for her he'd been kept him rooted to the spot. "I became a cop so I could carry a gun, so I could take control of whatever situation I found myself in. But standing on the other side of that iron gate tonight…" A pain registered in his chest, and his breath caught in his throat.

"I'm all right. Thanks to you, we're both all right."

He looked down at her hand on his arm, at her breasts just a few inches from his chest. It would be so easy to encircle her with his arms, to pull her close, to…

He forced his feet to step back. He couldn't play with fire. Not where Simone Jones was concerned. No matter how tempting. "You wouldn't have a drink, would you? I could use one. And I think you could, too."

Simone nodded. Tearing her gaze from his, she led the way down the hall. She crossed the living room to a wet bar along the far wall. Grabbing a crystal decanter, she poured amber liquid into two tumblers and held one out to him. "I hope you like bourbon."

"What self-respecting American doesn't?" He accepted the glass and took a good swig. The booze warmed his throat and calmed his racing pulse.

Simone emptied her glass before gesturing to the coffee table in the center of the room. "I found that on my doorstep. I'm assuming the woman who jumped me left it."

A dark glob stuck with black feathers lay on the glass tabletop. Liam drew a sharp breath. "Did you tell the cops about it?"

"Yes, but they didn't seem to think it was related,

so I dropped the subject. I figured it would do us more good to keep it.''

"Good thinking.'' He walked to the table. Leaning down, he studied the glob. "I talked to Camille's cousin, Cort DuPree, today. He may have *left* a voodoo charm like this one at Camille's door, but he didn't make it.''

"Who did?''

"He said a woman who referred to herself as a priest-ess called him and said the gods had told her he needed help. She promised to deliver a charm for him to leave on the doorstep of his enemy.''

She looked at him out of the corner of her eye, as if she knew what he was thinking. "Odette doesn't run around leaving threats on doorsteps.''

Liam set his glass on the table. "I know you want to write her off as a suspect, but I can't. Three people from her voodoo group are dead already.''

"DeLyon, Sadie Marceau and that woman who died a month ago.''

He nodded. "Janet Phillippe. And now you, Camille and Lisa Cantro have gotten charms. Not to mention that you and Camille were attacked.''

"Seems you're right about me becoming a target.''

"I wish I wasn't.'' He straightened, unable to keep his eyes from meeting hers.

In the brighter light of the living room, she looked stronger, more sure of herself. The Simone of the court-room again. A woman in command.

But this time he wasn't fooled. He'd seen the softness under her tough shell. And though she'd apparently re-covered from the shock of the attack, she was still in danger. Still in need of protection. If he needed evi-dence, he had only to drop his gaze a few inches to see the reddened outline of fingers on the tender skin of her neck. And even though his every nerve screamed for him to cut and run while he still had the ability to do so, he couldn't leave. He had to make sure she was safe.

He lowered himself to the couch. "I hope this thing is comfortable, because I'm spending the night."

SIMONE HANDED Liam a pillow and blanket, her fingers brushing his. A fluttery sensation raced along her nerves and settled in the pit of her stomach. She pulled her hand back.

She had to get a grip. She didn't know what unnerved her more—the attack she'd just survived or Liam's announcement that he was spending the night. But there was no denying she was unnerved. More unnerved than she'd ever been in her life.

"Well, good night, then," she said. "I guess I'll see you in the morning."

He nodded. "Do you have tomorrow free? Around lunchtime?"

"Jordan's bail hearing is scheduled at one."

Liam nodded. "Before that. Say eleven thirty."

Simone mentally scanned her schedule. "I don't have anything that can't be rescheduled."

"Then we have a lunch date."

The way he said the word *date* kicked the flutters in her stomach into a frenzy. She blocked the image of an intimate lunch with Liam and tried to match his all-business look with one of her own. "A lunch date?"

"With a friend of mine."

Disappointment congealed in her stomach. Ridiculous. She should be relieved they wouldn't be alone, shouldn't she? Dating the brother of a client couldn't be a good idea. And a button-down cop? She and Liam were as different as Creole and Cajun. But somehow relief was a feeling she couldn't quite manage. "Who?"

"René Badeaux. He's an assistant coroner."

Her disappointment abated. Of all the murder cases she'd defended in her career, she'd never gotten an up-close-and-personal meeting with a coroner to go over autopsy evidence. Having Liam work with her on this case was turning out to be intriguing on many levels. She gave him a measured nod, trying not to seem too enthusiastic about the meeting. "What restaurant?"

"We aren't exactly meeting in a restaurant."

"Where, then?"

"The morgue."

LIAM LAID two bags containing muffaletta sandwiches and black coffee on the stainless-steel counter at René Badeaux's elbow and tried not to look at the body his friend was bent over. As a cop, Liam had seen his fair share of stiffs, but that didn't mean he liked one as a centerpiece while he ate. The smell alone could kill any appetite.

Except René's. He looked up from his work, his round Cajun face testifying to his appetite's invincibility. He peeled off his gloves and nodded to the sandwiches. "You get them from Central Grocery?"

"Of course."

"Ah, my favorite." René glanced in Simone's direction. "You want to step out in the hall and talk? Your friend looks a little green."

Liam followed his gaze. The color of Simone's face had turned an unnatural shade, all right. Apparently she wouldn't be challenging René for the sandwiches, either.

They stepped into the hall. René joined them a few

moments later, bringing the food with him. "I looked up the cases you asked me to." He unwrapped a muffaletta.

"And?"

"DeLyon was poisoned with tetradotoxin, all right. And Sadie Marceau's throat was slit. But the third one, Janet Phillippe, she wasn't murdered at all."

Liam leaned forward. "What killed her?"

"She died of natural causes. In her case, heart failure." He took a giant bite of his sandwich.

"Could some kind of poison have caused her heart to fail?"

René held up a hand until he finished chewing. "Nope. She had a history of heart disease. Besides, the tox screens we did all came back negative."

"What did you test for?"

"You're thinking tetradotoxin, right?"

Liam nodded.

"No chance. We also tested for arsenic, cyanide, strychnine and nearly everything else you can think of."

Looking at René, Simone tilted her head. A crease of confusion marred her smooth forehead. "Do you usually do such exhaustive testing as part of the autopsy of an eighty-year-old woman who had heart disease?"

René shook his head. "We wouldn't usually do a tox screen at all. But in this case, the family insisted on it. Her daughter was convinced the old lady was murdered."

Simone's eyebrows dipped. "Why did she think that?"

René shrugged. "I remember her mentioning something about voodoo. To tell you the truth, I chalked her up as a nut."

Liam's mind raced. Maybe the woman wasn't as

much of a nut as René thought. Even though it appeared Janet Phillippe died of natural causes, who was to say she wasn't killed by voodoo? Or at least by the same person who was killing the other regulars at the voodoo ceremonies. "What else can you tell me, René?"

The Cajun glanced up and down the vacant hall. Apparently satisfied no one else was listening, he motioned Liam and Simone close. "I didn't tell you none of this, hear?"

Liam nodded.

"I did a little snooping for you on Jordan's case, and what I found wasn't good. Not good at all."

Liam braced himself. "Shoot."

"They have fingerprint evidence, Liam."

"They know Jordan was at both crime scenes. He told them that."

"Not just at the scenes. The fancy dagger the Marceau woman was killed with—it had his fingerprints on it. Expect him to be charged with her murder, too."

A weight descended on Liam's chest. His head throbbed. Jordan hadn't killed anyone. He'd stake his life on it. But with evidence like this, the truth might not matter. With evidence like this, Jordan might be on his way to death row regardless of his innocence.

Chapter Five

"The State of Louisiana versus Jordan O'Reilly. The charge is murder." The clerk's clipped bark echoed through the courtroom.

A rush of adrenaline pumped into Simone's bloodstream as it always did before she stepped inside the bar. She took her place at the podium just as a bailiff led Jordan to her side.

Dressed in a standard-issue prison jumpsuit, Jordan looked remarkably composed for a man facing the question of whether he would be free awaiting trial or stuck behind bars.

At the opposite table, an assistant district attorney who looked young even to Simone took a deep breath before launching into her spiel. "The state asks that the defendant be remanded, Your Honor. We feel he shouldn't get special privileges just because he's a police officer."

"Your Honor," Simone said, checking her impatience. "Bail isn't a special privilege. And I'd like the record to show that Jordan O'Reilly has asked for no special privileges."

"Maybe not," the assistant DA countered. "But we don't want any appearance of impropriety here. Besides, he's a flight risk. He was getting ready to flee when the detective in charge of the case arrested him.''

Simone cast the judge a dour look. "He was doing nothing of the kind. He was planning to turn himself in.''

"Is that why his brother is currently suspended from the police department for helping him escape?'' asked the assistant DA with a smile.

Simone shook her head. "Your Honor, it was all a misunderstanding fueled by the prejudice of the lead detect—''

The old curmudgeon on the bench held up a hand. "Save the conspiracy theories, Counselor. Bail is denied. The defendant will be remanded to the county jail to await trial.''

Simone shook her head. He couldn't cut her off. He had to let her argue her case. "But Your Honor—''

"That's enough, Ms. Jones. I've made my decision.''

Simone bit the inside of her cheek. Arguing with the judge wouldn't help her client. It would be better to concede this point and live to fight another day. She turned to Jordan. "I'm sorry.''

Jordan nodded. "Not much you could do. Judge Roth isn't known for his love of cops.''

A bailiff appeared beside Jordan. Before following the man back to the holding cell, Jordan touched her elbow. "Take care of Camille and Liam, would you, Simone? Especially Liam. Watching me go through this has got to be harder on him than going through it himself would be.''

She could understand the reason for Jordan's concern. At the morgue, Liam had taken the news of the fingerprint evidence against his brother hard. The seconds before his careful mask had slipped into place, he had turned as white as the body on the slab. Even without glancing back at the gallery, she was willing to bet Liam's color was worse now. "I'll take care of them."

With a final nod, Jordan let the bailiff lead him away.

Simone gathered her papers and briefcase and walked back through the center aisle and out of the courtroom.

Camille stood in the hall outside surrounded by a bodyguard, her family, Liam and an older couple who, judging from family resemblance, had to be Liam and Jordan's parents.

Simone joined the group. After a round of apologies and inquiries, she excused herself and strode down the hall.

Liam broke away and joined her. "You didn't have to apologize for anything, you know. Judge Roth would rather do jail time himself than give up the chance to stick it to a cop."

Simone nodded. She'd known her chances were slim, but it was still a relief to hear that Liam saw things the same way. She glanced back at the group they'd just left. "Camille puts on a brave face, but how is she really?"

"Shaken, but okay. She's finally agreed to leave her apartment and move to my parents' guest house. With the bodyguard Jordan arranged and my dad looking out for her, she'll be safe. She'll even be able to keep her restaurant open."

"So those *were* your parents. You sure look a lot like your dad."

A muscle jerked in Liam's jaw. "Yeah. A chip off the old block." He looked straight ahead.

Simone studied his profile. She'd love to know what caused his reaction, but she didn't dare ask. At least not right now. He'd been through more than enough for one day. He didn't need her probing on top of it. Although his emotions were tightly controlled and unreadable, his complexion was as pale as parchment. "How are you doing?"

"Great," Liam answered in a gruff voice. He angled his face away from her as they walked. "I'm planning to talk to some of the regulars at the voodoo ceremony this afternoon. Camille gave me photos at the hearing today, so I know who I'm looking for."

She nodded, still watching him. "Sounds like a logical next step."

"I'll drop you at your office on the way."

"Still worried about me?" she asked, trying to add a teasing lilt to her voice.

He glanced at her, not bothering to answer. "When will you be done with work?"

"Five-thirty or so." She glanced at her watch. She didn't have a late night tonight, but that still left four hours—four hours she wasn't sure Liam should spend alone. "On second thought, I don't have anything pressing today. I'll reschedule the entire afternoon."

"You sure?"

She shouldn't. She had reams of paperwork to fight through, not to mention preparing for Jordan's preliminary hearing. "I don't want to leave you alone. Not now."

A guarded look slipped into his eyes.

She fought the need to reach out, to touch him. "Hearing the evidence about Jordan must have been tough. And then to have him denied bail…"

He held up a hand. "I'm fine." Although his voice was strong, he didn't meet her eyes.

"Evidence isn't everything, you know."

"It's not? Is that what you plan to tell the jury?"

"Evidence can lead to the wrong conclusions. Or it can be wrong outright. And yes, that *is* what I'll tell the jury."

He let out a low sigh. "Wrong or not, they have enough to send Jordan to the state prison in Angola."

And death row, she mentally finished for him. "You're looking at this from the perspective of a police officer. There might be enough against him to press charges or even build a strong case. But trials don't work the same way. Evidence can be overcome."

"How? Through your lucky voodoo gris-gris?"

She ignored the sarcasm. It was natural for him to want to lash out. He cared about his brother. That was obvious. And he didn't like being out of his element. "A jury doesn't convict on evidence alone. They'll be able to see that he's innocent. I'll make sure they see it. All I need is for one juror to have reasonable doubt."

Again a muscle jumped in his jaw.

She reached out and laid a hand on his arm, which was rock hard under her fingers. She fought the urge to run her hand over the thin cotton of his dress shirt, to massage his tension away. The only thing she could do was try to reassure him. Try to put his mind at ease. "The most important thing is that you believe your brother is innocent. And continue to believe we'll find the answers we need to get him acquitted. Have faith."

"I don't believe in hunches and faith and luck. I believe in evidence."

"Even if the evidence says Jordan is guilty of murder?"

He pressed his lips into a bloodless line.

"You need to believe, Liam." Despite the warning blaring in her mind, she moved her hand up to his face and touched his jaw, the razor stubble teasing her fingertips. "If you let me, I'll help you learn."

THE COOL BLAST of air-conditioning hit Liam like a slap in the face as he opened the funeral parlor's door. The place felt as hushed and stagnant as a tomb. Rightly so, he supposed.

He held the door for Simone and followed her inside. They hadn't said a word to each other on the drive to the funeral home, which wasn't too far from the shores of Lake Pontchartrain. Even now, tension hovered between them. He could still feel her gentle touch, still hear her promise to help him learn to believe. And still feel the burning temptation to take her up on the offer.

He forced himself to focus on a set of open double doors down a short hall. He couldn't think about the woman beside him. Not about her touch or her promises and certainly not about how much he wanted to know her better. She had a way of turning on its head everything he knew to be true. And with his life already in turmoil, the last thing he needed was more. He needed to regain control. He needed to do his job, get some answers and move on. Elementary police work. Something he knew.

They stepped through the open doors and glanced around a large room. Judging from the rows of empty caskets, it was a showroom of sorts. And at the end of one row, Helen Gaylord was bent over a baby-blue steel number with silver accents and a silver satin lining.

Liam crossed to where she stood, Simone beside him. He hated disturbing Helen while she was mourning her sister, Sadie Marceau, but they had no choice.

A heavy woman with pronounced jowls, Helen

looked up at them with dry eyes. "Beautiful, isn't it? Sadie would have simply loved it."

He looked at the casket and nodded. "Yes. Beautiful."

"How much does it cost?"

Simone stepped toward the older woman. "We don't work here, Mrs. Gaylord," she said, her voice gentle. "We're here to ask you some questions."

"Miss," she corrected. "It's Miss Gaylord. Thanks to Sadie."

"Thanks to Sadie?" Liam echoed.

Helen nodded, still running her hand dreamily over the silver satin. "She stole my beau when I was twenty. He came to Mama and Papa's house to see me. And while he was waiting, she flirted with him so shamelessly he ended up smitten. I was so heartbroken, I never married."

Interesting. Here just days after Sadie's death, Helen Gaylord seemed more jealous than griefstricken. But then, who was to say what was normal? Liam had seen people react to the death of a loved one in a hundred different ways.

Simone's lips pinched with sympathy. "His loss, if you ask me, Miss Gaylord."

"Oh, call me Helen."

Simone smiled. "Can you tell us more about your sister, Helen?"

The older woman glanced from Simone to Liam and back again. "Who did you say you were?"

Liam tensed. Once Helen knew she was talking to Jordan's brother and lawyer, he doubted she'd be so forthcoming.

Simone leaned toward the woman. "We're trying to find out who killed your sister."

The corners of Helen's mouth turned down in a frown. "But the police said they arrested the man."

"Jordan O'Reilly didn't kill anyone." The words slipped out before Liam could bite them back.

Helen sighed. "Oh, I'm so relieved. He seemed like such a nice young man at the voodoo ceremony. So handsome. I didn't want to think…" Her gaze dropped back to the casket in front of her. She pulled a lacy handkerchief from her suitcase-size purse and dabbed her eyes, though Liam hadn't seen even the glint of a tear.

Simone touched the woman's arm in sympathy. "Not long after that last voodoo ceremony, Sadie called Camille DuPree. She said she knew something about Spiro DeLyon's death. Do you know what that could be?"

Helen shook her head, her jowls wagging with the movement. "She never told me anything. I was just her spinster sister. No reason to confide important things to me."

"Might it have something to do with the voodoo rituals the two of you attended together?" Liam asked, adopting Simone's sympathetic tone.

"I don't know. Maybe."

Simone's turn. "Did she receive any kind of a voodoo charm before her death?"

Helen shook her head. "Have you talked to Miss Lulu? Did she tell you about the charm?"

Liam tensed. "Mrs. DeLyon received a charm?"

"Not her. Someone left one of the ugly things at Spiro's office the day he died. At least that's what I heard. If you want to know more, you'll have to talk to Miss Lulu herself. She'll be at the Saenger Theatre tonight. She asked Sadie and me to join her and Spiro before…" Once again she raised the handkerchief to catch phantom tears. "She might be able to carry on with her theater plans after what's happened, but I just can't."

A thin man in a dark suit joined them. His approach had been so silent Liam hadn't noticed him until he was but a few steps away. The man gave Helen a somber smile. "This is a very beautiful casket," he said in a hushed voice. "From what you've told me, I really believe it would be perfect for your sister."

Helen raised her head as if snapped from a trance. She looked down her nose at the funeral director and shook her head. "No. I think a plain wood one would be better for Sadie. But I'd like to reserve this one for myself. All of us die eventually, you know. And I want to be prepared."

New Orleans's Saenger Theatre stood like a dusty old jewel on the edge of the French Quarter. Liam had passed it countless times in his patrols and day-to-day life, but he'd never stepped inside until now.

The place was just as he'd imagined. Ornate decor with Greek and Roman sculpture, marble statues and cut-glass chandeliers set the scene for a crowd dressed in everything from somber black gowns to sequins and feather boas.

Simone fit right in.

Dressed in a high-neck black halter dress with an elaborate brooch pinned at the throat, she glided through the crowd beside him. Her back was bare to her waist, exposing creamy skin. Her hair was swept up and a few blond curls framed her face. Stunning.

He shifted uncomfortably in his tux.

Suddenly Simone stopped walking. There at one of the bars in the lobby stood a woman who had to be

Lulu DeLyon. She wore a turquoise dress that was so beaded it looked as if it was made of chain mail. Her bright-red hair was piled high on top of her head, and her fingers were laden with a fortune in rings. She held a champagne flute in each bejeweled hand. Turning from the bar, she searched the crowd as if looking for someone.

Simone glanced up at him. "Do you want the first shot at her?"

He'd seen Simone in action questioning Helen. Seen her patience, her gentleness, her compassion. The elderly woman had responded to her like an old friend. Maybe Miss Lulu would respond the same way. "Be my guest."

Simone headed her quarry off at the end of the bar, Liam right behind her. "Excuse me, Mrs. DeLyon?" Simone smiled up at the taller woman, her nose wrinkling disarmingly.

"Call me Miss Lulu. Everybody does. And you are?"

Simone stuck her hand out. "Simone Jones."

Miss Lulu's eyes narrowed. "You're his lawyer." She turned to Liam. "And you're his brother, aren't you? The detective warned me about both of you."

Warned her? Damn Yancy. The pompous son of a bitch would stop at nothing.

Simone waved her words aside as if the whole thing was merely a misunderstanding. "We just want to ask you a few questions. Nothing worthy of a warning."

Miss Lulu raised her chin and peered down her nose at Simone. "You want to ask questions so you can get Spiro's murderer out of jail."

"My brother didn't kill your husband, Miss Lulu," Liam said.

"No? Then why is he in jail?"

"Detective Yancy arrested the wrong man," Simone said. "The real murderer is still out there. And we need your help to catch him. Or *her*."

Miss Lulu's skin went chalky under the heavy makeup.

Liam stepped toward her. "Did your husband receive a voodoo charm the day before he died? A dark-brown lump stuck with feathers?"

The widow's lips flattened. "Where did you hear that?"

"It's an evil charm, Miss Lulu," Liam continued. "An omen of death."

Her eyes widened.

"Others connected to Odette LaFantary's voodoo ceremonies have received charms, as well. *After* my brother was arrested."

"Are you saying that Odette killed Spiro? I don't believe it."

Simone glanced at Liam, then back to Miss Lulu. "I don't believe it was Odette, either. But someone left the charms. Someone who is out there right now waiting to deliver on the threats."

Miss Lulu swallowed hard. Raising her chin even more, she tried to cover her fear.

Liam wasn't fooled. "Maybe you want to sit back and listen to Detective Yancy. Maybe you believe he'll protect you. But three people connected with the voodoo group have already died. If the real murderer's objective is to kill all the regulars at Odette LaFantary's voodoo ceremonies, can you take the chance you won't be next?"

Her hand fluttered to her throat. She looked away

from them as if searching for someone in the crowd to come to her aid.

"Please, Miss Lulu," Simone said. "Help us and help yourself."

Miss Lulu's searching gaze stilled, as if she'd found the person she was looking for. Taking a deep breath, she drew herself up and looked Simone straight in the eye. "Detective Yancy said I don't have to answer to defense counsel and I don't intend to. It's time for me to go to my seat. If you'll excuse me." With that, she turned and headed off.

SIMONE WATCHED Miss Lulu join the crowd filing into the theater auditorium. They had been close. So close. "She was about to talk. Until she found whoever it was she was looking for."

Liam nodded. He glanced at the stairs behind them, the marble railings sweeping upstairs to the balcony. "Let's go see who it is." He grasped Simone's hand and started up the stairs.

Heat shot through her at the feel of his hand holding hers. Trying to keep her mind on Miss Lulu, instead of the rough strength of his fingers, she followed him up the stairs to the second floor. But before he could lead her into the seating area, she stopped in her tracks. "Wait. I know where we can get a better view without being spotted."

Giving his fingers a squeeze, she led him to a side staircase and began to climb. When they reached the next floor, instead of heading for the doors leading to the back of the balcony, she walked to an isolated door that resembled the wrought-iron gate at the side of the theater. She grabbed the handle and pulled. It creaked open and they ducked inside.

Liam followed her into a narrow hall with dusty cement floors. Twinkling lights sparkled like stars in the theater's ceiling, only ten feet over their heads. On one side, the hall opened to a balcony lined with Greek statuary. Standing behind the naked torso of a woman, they peered over the edge.

The gallery yawned beneath them. Liam glanced at Simone. ''We can see everyone in the theater from here. How did you know about this place?''

She shot him a sly smile. ''What can I say? I've always enjoyed watching the performances that aren't on the stage.'' She dipped her hand into her purse and pulled out a pair of opera glasses. Holding them to her eyes, she scanned the crowd. It didn't take long to locate Miss Lulu's bright hair. And from the photo Camille had provided, it didn't take much longer to recognize the dark hair and slight build of the man sitting next to her. ''There she is. Middle section, about a third of the way back on the aisle. And you'll never guess who she's with.'' She handed Liam the glasses.

He held them to his eyes. ''Tony Fortune.''

Even without the glasses, Simone saw the man slip his arm over the back of the theater seat and pull Miss Lulu close as the curtain rose.

Liam closed his eyes. After a moment, he opened them and handed the opera glasses back to Simone. ''So much for voodoo. I guess DeLyon was just in the way.'' He bit off the words, his voice strangely harsh.

Simone studied him out of the corner of her eye. ''They do seem pretty friendly.''

''Especially when her husband's body won't even be put in the crypt until tomorrow.'' Unmistakable bitterness laced his voice. Bitterness coming from who knew where? Simone wondered. "We've seen all we need to. Let's get out of here."

She grabbed his arm. "Not until you tell me what's going on."

"What do you mean?"

"I can't see you getting this upset about Miss Lulu's infidelities. What's the real reason?"

Blowing a breath through tight lips, he shook his head. "It doesn't matter. It all happened a long time ago."

"Tell me. If something's bothering you, I want to know what it is."

He looked away from her, studying the little lights in the ceiling. Finally he said, "My father had an affair."

She nodded. Only some personal hurt would account for the bitterness in his tone. "How long ago?"

"Before I was born. When he and my mother were engaged."

She couldn't hide her surprise. "Before you were born? Don't you think it's time you got over it, Liam?"

"It's not that simple." He turned to look at her, his green eyes shrouded, as if he was trying to hide old hurts, old betrayals. "He had a child with his French mistress. His firstborn son. Until I was seventeen, I thought *I* was his firstborn son."

Simone ran her hand down his arm. She wished she could say something to make things better, to make things different. But she knew those words didn't exist. All she could do was listen. And try to understand. "I grew up an army brat. My whole world changed every time my father was transferred to a new base."

"It's not the same thing."

"Of course it's not. But I do understand. At least a little." She fought the urge to touch him again. She couldn't heal his hurt no matter what she said or did. He'd have to do that on his own. "Do you know your brother?"

"My half brother, you mean."

"Do you know him?"

"Yeah."

"Have you talked to him about it?"

Liam held up a hand as if shielding himself. "Listen. I answered your question. I'm not going to talk about it anymore. I have to go make sure my *real* brother's fiancée hasn't slipped her bodyguards and decided she's going to clear Jordan herself, and this damn phone won't work in here." He held up his cell phone as if showing her proof, then turned, walked through the wrought-iron door and made a beeline for the stairs.

Simone watched his retreating back.

SIMONE STEPPED OUT of the theater and into the humid night. The curls framing her face stuck to her forehead immediately. She scanned the sidewalk. Liam was nowhere in sight. Nor had she been able to find him inside.

Her stomach knotted with disappointment. She'd been attracted to Liam since the first time she'd cross-examined him in court. And ever since they'd started working together on Jordan's defense, her attraction for the no-nonsense cop had grown by leaps and bounds. She'd even gone so far as to fantasize there was something deeper between them. Or at least hope there could be. Something that transcended their differences. Something she'd been searching for all her life.

She shook her head. Maybe Liam was right. Maybe she was trying to believe in myths. Maybe the elusive something she'd thought was between them was nothing more than another of those myths. He'd certainly had no trouble walking away from her tonight.

She started to cross Burgundy Street before she realized what she was doing. She was so used to walking everywhere she wanted to go in the French Quarter, she'd momentarily forgotten about being attacked in her courtyard last night. Spotting a cab approaching down Canal Street, she raised a hand to hail it. Even though her house was only a few blocks away, she'd be smarter to take a cab than face the walk alone. But the cab, already filled with bead-wearing tourists who didn't realize Mardi Gras was long over, passed her by.

"Simone." A voice rang out over the sound of light traffic and music drifting from a distant street corner. Liam's voice.

Stopping in the street, she turned to face him. Her heart hammered high in her chest.

He strode toward her, his face flushed. "I want to apologize. I was an idiot back there." He stepped off the curb.

The squeal of rubber on pavement ricocheted off surrounding buildings. A car careered into the neutral ground in the middle of Canal Street and screeched around the corner. It straightened and raced directly at them.

His back to the car, Liam didn't see it coming.

"Liam!" Simone lunged for him.

Chapter Six

Liam fell backward, Simone landing on top of him. Air exploded from his lungs. He gasped for breath, for thought.

The car had nearly hit them! Nearly killed them both. He hadn't seen it, hadn't heard it. If Simone hadn't reacted so quickly, they'd both be dead.

He wrapped his arms around her, holding her tightly. Her racing heartbeat matched his.

"Are you okay?" Pulling back, she looked down at him, eyes wide with alarm, with concern. Concern for him.

He slid a hand up her silky back and cradled her head. His lips skimmed her forehead, her cheek, that cute little nose. Finally he found her lips.

A moan sounded from deep in her throat. A moan that echoed the desire, the need that cramped his own chest.

He deepened the kiss, wanting to taste all of her, wanting to convince himself that they were both alive.

She opened her lips, letting him inside, tangling her tongue with his. Her arms tightened around him. Her body pressed down on his.

Desire slammed through him, carried by adrenaline.

He'd never felt this way before. Never needed a woman this much. Never been this far out on the edge. He moved his hands over her bare back.

He couldn't do this.

He ended the kiss and sat up, still holding Simone, unwilling to let her go just yet. "We have to report this."

Simone nodded. She pulled away from him and struggled to her feet.

Though the night was warm, cold air rushed to fill the spot her warmth had been. He stood. He couldn't think about how his arms ached to reach for her, to pull her back against his chest.

Instead, he pulled out his cell phone and called the station. After reporting the attempted hit-and-run, he asked the dispatcher to send someone to the theater. A few minutes later, a police car pulled to the curb beside them. A blue-uniformed officer stepped from the car.

Liam stiffened.

Although he worked out of the same station house as Zachary Doucet, he avoided his half brother whenever possible. Doucet resembled an O'Reilly far too much for Liam's comfort. He even walked like an O'Reilly. And if Liam was honest, Doucet's intense green eyes looked as much like their father's as did his own and Jordan's.

Doucet narrowed those green eyes as he assessed the situation. "What seems to be the problem, O'Reilly?"

Liam gritted his teeth at the emphasis Doucet put on his last name.

Simone glanced at Liam as if wondering why he didn't answer, then focused on Doucet. "A car tried to run us down. A burgundy sedan."

"You didn't happen to notice the make or model, did you, ma'am?" A hint of an accent caressed each word.

She shook her head. "It all happened too fast."

"Then I don't suppose you got a license number."

Anger stirred in Liam's gut. Seeing Miss Lulu and Tony together in the theater had been a bitter reminder of his father's betrayal. Having to deal with Doucet and his French charm tonight of all nights was more than he could take. "She said it happened too fast to notice a make or model. Do you really think she had time to see the license number?"

Doucet arched a brow.

Simone gave Liam a surprised look of her own. She glanced to Doucet. Realization dawned in her eyes. "You're Liam's half brother."

Doucet said nothing. He merely watched Liam, as if waiting to see if he'd claim him.

A bitter lump formed in Liam's throat. He'd resented Doucet from the moment he'd learned his half brother existed—eleven long years ago. Jordan had never harbored such resentment. Even their mother had long since moved on. Maybe Simone was right. Maybe it was time he moved on, as well. At least, maybe it was time to try.

Liam dragged in a breath. "Simone, this is Zachary Doucet. My father's other son. His oldest son."

Simone nodded. "Nice to meet you, Zachary."

Doucet stared at Liam as if stunned. A guarded look slipped into his eyes, as if Liam's acknowledgment was some kind of cruel joke. He looked down at Simone. "Nice to meet you."

"Jordan is in jail, charged with two murders," Liam said.

"I heard. He's my brother, too, after all."

"If you really want to be his brother, you'll do whatever you can to help clear him. Starting with protecting his lawyer." He nodded to Simone.

"Be glad to." Doucet's smile was gracious, but the tone of his voice was still guarded, still not buying into Liam's change of heart. Before he could say more, another car pulled up behind Doucet's. Yancy and Rebecca Romero climbed out and approached them.

Doucet watched Romero with heavy-lidded eyes. If Liam remembered correctly, the two of them had been partners once, before Romero had been promoted to detective. If she'd known the promotion meant partnering with Yancy, maybe she would have reconsidered taking it.

Yancy straightened his French cuffs and swaggered toward them. "You can go, Doucet. We'll take care of this."

Doucet bristled at Yancy's dismissal. If Liam wasn't mistaken, he'd swear his half brother wanted a piece of Yancy as much as he did.

Rebecca Romero cleared her throat. "Thank you, Officer Doucet."

Doucet's gaze snapped to his former partner. After a long moment, he heaved a breath, turned away and strode to his car.

Yancy's eyes narrowed on Liam. "So what's this all about, O'Reilly? Dispatch said something about a hit-and-run."

Liam filled Yancy in on their close call with the sedan.

The detective scowled. "And you expect us to give the two of you protection?"

"Last I checked, that was part of the job."

"Last I checked, cars come close to hitting pedestrians about forty times a night around here."

"This wasn't just a random close call," Liam said.

"You have evidence of that?"

Simone stepped into Yancy's path. "We have eyewitness evidence, Detective."

"And where's the witness?"

"Us. The car accelerated and headed straight for us."

Yancy brushed an imaginary piece of dust from his designer duds and shook his head. "I'm afraid that's not good enough, Miz Jones. We don't have the manpower to offer protection to everyone who was almost hit by a car."

She tilted her head. "Even if the attempt is tied to the voodoo murders?"

Yancy's face turned pink, a shade lighter than his tie. "Damn reporters and their sensational headlines. Those murders were caused by nothing but a dirty cop settling an old score and covering his tracks. Not voodoo."

Liam balled his hands into fists by his sides. "Jordan didn't kill anybody, Yancy. If you were more concerned with doing your job than impressing the promotions board, you'd see that."

Yancy scoffed. "Your brother is a hotheaded dirty cop. It's time you realized that, O'Reilly, and quit defending him." He turned to Simone. "If someone comes after you with a gun or knife, give me a call. Otherwise, don't tie up the station's resources."

Liam bit back a curse. He'd never been one to lose his temper, but tonight he felt like blowing up at the world. Instead, he looked at Romero. He'd noticed her hesitation to follow Yancy before. Surely, under the circumstances, she could see that Simone should be protected. But whether she would go against Yancy was another question.

She fingered the gold cross hanging from the chain around her neck as if struggling with the question. Finally she turned and followed Yancy to the car.

Liam heaved a sigh. "Looks like we're on our own."

"So what happens now?" Simone looked up at him.

What *did* happen now? "I'll find a way to protect you. I'll find a way to make sure you're safe."

"I have a couch that's free." Her lips parted slightly as if she was remembering their kiss. The blue of her eyes seemed to deepen, to draw him in. "Unless you don't want to sleep on the couch tonight."

Need jolted through Liam's system. He'd give anything to share Simone's bed, to run his hands over her soft skin, to bury himself—

He shook his head. He couldn't be anywhere near Simone tonight, and he knew it. Even as he stood on the street corner talking to her now, the urge to take her in his arms nearly overwhelmed him.

"I'll stand guard tonight in your courtyard," he said at last. "No one will get near you."

No one—including him.

SIMONE PEERED out her bedroom window at the courtyard below. She couldn't see Liam. The corner where he sat by the fountain was hidden by the wide leaves of banana and branches of magnolia. But she didn't have to see him to feel his presence.

The events of the night spun through her mind. Liam's pain when he spoke of his father's infidelity and secret son. The fear that had stabbed her at the sight of the car speeding toward him. The warmth of his arms and the heady flavor of his kiss. The way he was protecting her now.

She knew why he wouldn't come inside. If he did, there wasn't a chance he'd sleep on the couch tonight. Not if she had anything to say about it. The more she saw of Liam O'Reilly, the more she wanted him, and the more she wanted to believe the connection between them was real.

If only she could convince him to open up. To explore what was between them. To throw caution to the wind and believe as well.

She blew a curl off her forehead. Fat chance she had of doing that. The man would never give up his iron-fisted control. Hell, he wouldn't even step foot in her house.

She glanced around the kitchen, her gaze landing on the coffeemaker. A smile stole over her lips. She didn't have to wait for him to venture inside. She could go to him.

AN ALMOST IMPERCEPTIBLE sound nicked the quiet of Simone's courtyard.

Liam straightened in the wrought-iron chair, his hand automatically finding the .22 he'd laid on the table in front of him. He sat very still, straining his ears to listen.

The sound came again, the click of a door latch releasing. A figure slipped out of the house. *Simone.* She was still wearing the black dress, but her hair was loose around her shoulders. Light from the converted gas lamps shimmered in her curls and reflected off the cups and coffee carafe in her hands.

Liam set the gun back on the table, but he didn't relax. If anything, the knot in his gut tightened.

If the sound had come from an intruder, he would

have known what to do. But Simone? He had no idea what to do with her. Not if he wanted to keep his sanity.

"I thought you might like some coffee." She set the pot and cups on the table and sank into the chair beside him. As she moved close, her scent eclipsed that of the coffee and the flowers around them—sweeter, richer, more intoxicating.

He leaned toward her before he caught himself. Gripping the chair arms, he forced himself to remain seated. "I told you to stay inside where I can be sure you're safe."

"I don't follow orders well." Her lips quirked into a smile, her nose wrinkling that irresistible way. "Besides, I'm plenty safe out here with you and your gun."

She might be teasing, but she was right. With the high stone walls around them and the front gate secured by a chain and padlock, no one could slip into the courtyard without his knowing about it. He wanted Simone sequestered to keep her out of his sight. To keep from feeling what he was feeling now. "I have a hard time controlling myself when you're around."

She leaned toward him. "What would be so bad about losing control, Liam? What would be so bad about finding out what could be between us?"

He drew in a breath. He wanted to know. His whole body ached to know. But he couldn't risk it. "You do something to me. I don't think straight when I'm around you."

"I feel the same way."

He searched her face, trying to read if she was teasing again. "You really mean that, don't you?"

"Does it surprise you?"

"Yes."

"Why?"

"You're so spontaneous, so alive. I'm not that way at all. I could never be that way."

"Maybe that's one of the things I like about you." She tilted her head. "I moved around so much as a kid that I've never felt grounded. Maybe in some way, you ground me." She raised a hand to his face and traced his lips with a gentle finger.

A shiver worked over his skin. He felt anything but grounded. Around Simone he felt off balance and vital and shaken to the core.

"I've never felt at home anywhere. Not until I met you." She moved her finger over his lower lip and settled it in the cleft of his chin. "The day we went to Odette's, I told you I was looking for something to believe in. Well, Liam, I think I've found it. I believe in you. I believe in the magic between us. I want you to believe, too."

He leaned toward her. His hand found her shoulder and slipped under her curls to cradle the back of her neck. He wanted to believe. Hell, he wanted Simone. More than he'd wanted anything in his life. Before he knew what he was doing, he lowered his head and fitted his lips to hers.

She tasted as sweet and exotic as her scent. And he hungered for more. He rose from his chair, pulling her against the length of his body.

She opened her mouth to his kiss. Her arms circled his neck. Twining one leg around his, she pulled him closer, nestling him between her thighs, melting against him.

He couldn't get enough of her. Her taste, her scent, the feel of her body, fragile and strong at the same time. He smoothed his hand over the silk of her back. Reaching the clasp at her nape, he released it and lowered the dress to her waist.

She wasn't wearing a bra, and her breasts glowed white in the gas lamp's light. Her nipples puckered as if begging for his touch.

He molded a hand over one supple mound. Lowering his head, he drew the erect nipple into his mouth and circled it with his tongue.

She was sweet, intoxicating. He moved to the other breast, caressing and suckling. And when he'd thoroughly lavished both, he slipped her dress over her hips and let it puddle on the cobblestone. Her panties followed. Gentle light glowed off her skin, making her so beautiful she seemed otherworldly. He smoothed his hands down her sides and over the swell of her buttocks until he found the source of her heat.

A moan sounded from deep in her throat. She moved against him, her breath quickening. Finally she gasped and shattered under his touch.

He buried a finger in her warmth and claimed her lips, kissing her deeply. He couldn't get enough of her. He could never get enough.

Regaining her breath, she kissed him back. Her fingers found the buttons of his shirt. One by one, she worked them free. When she reached the bottom of the shirt, she moved to his pants, unbuttoning, unzipping. She slipped her hands under his waistband, under his briefs, and eased them down.

He sprang free, hard with desire. She closed a hand over his length, stroking until he thought he'd explode.

He grabbed her wrist, stopping the movement of her hand.

"Let go, Liam. Let go and believe."

He kissed her lips, still holding her wrists. He couldn't let go. If he did—

"Let go. I won't bite." Her nose wrinkled. "Much."

A chuckle bubbled from his throat. Dragging in a deep breath, he released her wrists.

She brought her hands up to rest on his shoulders, then pushed him down to the stone floor and placed her hands against his chest. Caressing his skin, she eased him back. He leaned against the edge of the fountain, the moss soft and cool on his hot skin.

She moved over him, straddling his waist. Her nipples grazed his chest. Starting with his mouth, she littered kisses down his chest and over his belly. Then she moved lower. Finally she took him in her mouth.

Desire surged through him, making him dizzy. She stroked and teased with her tongue, the heat in him building, bursting into flame.

Just when he was sure he was a goner, she kissed her way back up his belly and chest to his mouth. She rose over him, her breasts swinging above. He took a nipple into his mouth, suckling, kissing, devouring.

She worked a hand between their sweaty bodies. Fitting him to her, she slowly sank onto him.

He surged into her softness. They settled into a rhythm, the heat building, the need growing, overwhelming. Until there was nothing except her and the heat and the magic. Until he couldn't help but believe.

Chapter Seven

Simone awoke to the morning sun pouring through her bedroom window. She glanced at the clock. A quarter to seven and it was no doubt already hot and humid outside. A typical June day in New Orleans. But no matter how high the temperature climbed, nothing could be as sultry as last night. A smile curved her lips. She didn't have to look to know Liam was still behind her in bed, still asleep. His fingers rested on her hip. The soft caress of his breath tickled her neck.

After the passion they'd shared in the courtyard, she'd convinced him they'd both be safer and more comfortable if they spent the rest of the night in her bed. And although they hadn't gotten much sleep, the decision had been a good one. Moss and summer night air might be nice, but nothing beat a bed. A bed and Liam. What more could she want?

She rolled over and looked into his eyes. "You're awake."

"Yes."

Excitement shivered through her. She leaned close and kissed him on the mouth. "Let's stay in bed and make love all day."

"We can't. You have work to do. And so do I."

She nodded. He was right of course. But hearing him say it made her feel as subdued as he sounded. ''I need to meet with Jordan,'' she said. ''I'm going to recommend he waive the preliminary hearing. The last thing we need is for the media to learn what evidence the state has against him and spread the word. This case is going to be tough enough without them poisoning the jury pool further.''

''Sounds like a good strategy.''

''So what are you doing today?'' She flinched inwardly at the clingy sound in her voice. Except in her law practice, she never believed in keeping a strict schedule, let alone holding someone else to one. But for the first time in her life, she wanted every moment planned so she'd know exactly how long it would be before she saw him again.

''DeLyon's funeral is late this afternoon. I want to see who shows up.''

''Will that be over in time for us to grab a bite? Or would you rather skip eating and spend the night back here?''

She looked into his eyes. But instead of the warmth and love and blatant desire she craved, his gaze was shuttered. Controlled.

A chill worked over her skin. ''What is it?''

He looked away.

''Liam, what's wrong?''

A muscle flexed in his jaw. ''Nothing.''

Fear streaked through her. ''Do you regret last night?''

He moved his hands as if trying to erase her words. ''No. Last night was incredible.''

''But?'' She held her breath, fearing what would come next but unable to stop it. She'd felt his reservations since she'd awakened. She just hadn't wanted to acknowledge them. "It was incredible, but you don't want it to happen again."

He sat up in bed, the sheet falling to his waist, exposing his broad chest. "It's not that. I just..." He pressed his lips together.

"You just what?" Simone struggled to keep her voice even.

"Everything has happened so fast. I need some time. I need to think."

"So think. It's okay. We can slow things down, get to know each other."

He swung his legs over the side of the bed. Facing away from her, he raked an agitated hand through his hair. "I can't think when I'm around you. I need some time alone."

There it was. Just what she'd feared. If it truly was a matter of his needing time, she wouldn't be so worried. But it wasn't that simple. She knew as surely as she knew anything that Liam was pulling away from her. Withdrawing into the self-protective mode he'd probably been in since he was seventeen. "My closets are empty, Liam."

"What?"

"No skeletons. You see what you get. You don't have to worry about something turning up, throwing your world into chaos."

He shook his head. "I'm not worried about skeletons. You throw my world into chaos every time you're near."

"And that's why—"

He held up a hand. "No. That's not why I need time. I love your spontaneity, your fire."

"Then what is it?"

He sat still for a long time, tension bunching the muscles in his back. Finally he said, "I grew up feeling the distance between my mom and dad, the tension. It was there even before my mom knew about the affair and about Zachary. I don't want that kind of distance between us. I never want to see that fire in your eyes turn cold."

"Judging from last night, I don't think we have to worry about that." She tried to force levity into her voice, but the attempt fell flat.

"Last night was only one night. What if things change? What if someone ends up hurt?"

"I won't hurt you, Liam."

"I'm not worried about myself."

Her heart felt pinched. "I'm tough. You know that."

He rubbed a hand over his face. "I don't know if I believe in lasting love, Simone. I sure haven't seen any evidence of it in my lifetime."

"And you never will unless you take a chance." She touched his shoulder. His skin was warm and smooth over hard muscle. She longed to move her hands over his body as she had last night, to banish tension and doubt. But she couldn't. Not if he wouldn't let her. "What we had last night was magic, Liam. Don't throw it away."

"I'm not throwing anything away. I just need time to think."

"You can have time." She choked back a surge of tears. "And when you're done thinking, I'll be here. Just don't take too long."

He nodded but didn't look at her.

Despair sank into her chest like a rusty blade.

LIAM STOOD in the doorway of an art gallery and stared across Dauphine Street at Simone's courtyard gate.

Even though the security guard he'd hired was sitting in the courtyard keeping watch, Liam couldn't stay away. He'd replayed last night in his mind all day. All through DeLyon's funeral and interment in St. Louis Cemetery No. 1., his thoughts had been on Simone. Her vitality. Her spontaneity. Her warmth. More than anything he wanted to cross the street, storm into her house, take her in his arms and never let her go.

He leaned his forehead against the rough stone archway. What he'd told her this morning had been true. Everything between them had happened too fast. He needed time to absorb it. To analyze it. To make sure he was doing the right thing for him and for her. He couldn't live with the idea of hurting her or, worse, trapping her in a relationship that turned cold. Of watching the spontaneity and the life drain out of her the way it had drained out of his mother.

He was doing the right thing. He was sure of it.

Then why was he lurking in a doorway in the middle of the night watching her house like some kind of stalker?

He shook his head and stood his ground. He couldn't surrender to his feelings, and he had to make sure she was safe. Watching her house from the other side of the street was the only way he could do both.

A flash of light from Simone's courtyard caught his eye. The shimmer of blond hair in shadow.

He straightened. His hand found his gun.

The gate swung open. Simone stepped out, followed by the security guard. She turned to talk to the man.

Liam strained to hear her. All that reached his ears was music drifting up from Bourbon Street. If only he could read lips.

Finishing the conversation, Simone stepped off the banquette and crossed the street.

Liam retreated into shadow. He gritted his teeth. What the hell was she doing? And how had she convinced the security guard to let her traipse around the streets alone in the middle of the night?

He tensed as she drew closer. He would have to follow her after she passed. He was going to make damn sure she was safe, no matter what she had in mind.

But instead of passing, she stopped in front of the gallery's doorway. Tilting her head, she squinted into the darkness. "Liam?"

He stepped out of the doorway. "What the hell are you doing out here?"

"I could ask you the same thing."

"I wanted to make sure you were safe."

"Then come with me."

"Where?"

"To Bourbon Street. I did a little snooping into Tony Fortune's habits today. He hangs out at a bar on Bourbon. The bartender just gave me a call. It seems Tony stopped in for a few on his way to a voodoo ceremony. Interested?"

He was plenty interested. "Lead the way."

It didn't take long to walk the block to Bourbon Street. Small groups of people milled around and strolled down the street from bar to bar, plastic "go" cups in their hands. Nightclub doors gaped open, music spilling out. Liam followed Simone into a small bar where a piano player pounded out blues in the tradition of Professor Longhair.

He spotted Tony Fortune at the far side of the bar. Well on his way to drunkenness, Fortune swayed on his stool, slurring words as he talked to a tourist perched next to him.

Simone slid onto a stool and nodded to the bartender.

The bartender crossed to them immediately. "Hey, Simone. You made it in time." He smiled at her, the kind of smile Liam knew he himself had worn more than once while looking at her. He hated the guy immediately.

Simone nodded. "Thanks for the tip. I owe you one."

The bartender's smile grew wider. No doubt he was thinking of ways she could pay him back. "What can I get you?"

"A couple of beers."

The bartender set two bottles of local brew on the bar, collected the bills Liam threw him, and moved on to another customer.

Simone wrapped her fingers around her bottle, her eyes on Tony Fortune. "He's about my height, wouldn't you say? And he probably doesn't weigh much more."

Liam sized up the man. He was pretty sure where Simone was heading. "The same size as the person who attacked you."

"And the same size as Camille's voodoo priestess."

"It's possible." Liam watched Fortune, trying to envision him in dark clothing and a mask. But his eyes kept wandering to Simone. It was all he could do to keep from reaching out and touching her jean-clad leg. He forced himself to grasp his beer bottle, instead.

On the other side of the room, Tony Fortune climbed off his stool and onto unsteady legs. He wove across the dance floor and stepped outside. Liam and Simone slipped out the door after him.

Fortune's dark head bobbed among the throngs of tourists. But instead of continuing down Bourbon Street with the rest of the crowd, he turned up Conti.

Liam and Simone dropped farther back to avoid being spotted.

Fortune wove up the street until he reached Basin and the gates of St. Louis Cemetery No. 1. He entered the cemetery, Liam and Simone behind.

Once inside the gates, Liam spotted Odette immediately. Holding a candle, she wore a white dress and a white cloth wrapped around her head. She stood in front of one of the crypts, speaking in low tones. A group of four gathered around her. Dressed similarly but in black and purple, instead of white, they stood with heads bowed, candles in their hands. Tony Fortune joined the group. In the flickering light, Liam could make out red and black marks on the white stone behind them.

"This is the tomb of Marie Laveau," Odette said in a low voice. "We are here tonight to ask that she and the Gede—the gods of death and cemeteries—protect the souls of those who have joined the City of the Dead today. And bring to us the murderer of Spiro DeLyon and Sadie Marceau so he or she will face justice."

Odette turned and walked farther into the cemetery. The group followed. When she stopped again, it was in front of a large crypt with the name DeLyon carved into the granite. Liam and Simone ducked behind a nearby sarcophagus.

Dipping her hand into a bag by her side, Odette held aloft a child's tiny shoe. "To this shoe I will add the dust from around Spiro DeLyon's grave. Children have tender minds, minds that are easily led. And when we burn this child's shoe in prayer, the gods will lead the murderer back to this victim. Back to face justice."

"Odette said she was going to do something to stop the killer," Simone whispered. "This must be what she meant." She glanced at him. A curl draped over her forehead and dangled in her eyes.

He raised his hand to brush the strand back from her face, but then let it fall back to his side. What was he thinking? He didn't dare touch Simone. Not unless he wanted to drive them both crazy. The fact was, he wasn't thinking. He could never think when she was around. When she was around, he wanted only to feel and love and lose control.

Still watching him, she reached out and brushed his fingers, as if offering her hand.

He didn't take it. He couldn't, no matter how much he wanted to. Tearing his eyes from her, he focused on what Odette was doing.

The voodoo priestess knelt at the foot of the crypt and set on the ground the candle she was holding. The other five followed suit. The flames of six candles illuminated Odette's hand as she collected a pinch of dirt from the base of the tomb. Sifting the dust between finger and thumb, she deposited it in the tiny shoe.

She rose to her feet, leaving the others clustered around the candles. Slowly she moved around the tomb, gathering more dust, each time adding it to the shoe. Her seemingly wordless chant drifted through the still air, melodious, beseeching.

Liam moved behind a closer sarcophagus, trying to get an unobstructed view. To his relief, Simone stayed where she was.

Finally the priestess returned to the front of the tomb. She pulled a small cloth bag from her satchel and added its contents to the dirt in the shoe. Then taking the candle she'd left at the tomb's entrance, she held it to the baby shoe until it caught fire.

The fire's light flickered over Odette's face. Deep shadows collected in the hollows of her cheeks. She chanted faster, her voice rising and falling. The small shoe crackled and curled in the flame. She set it among the candles at the foot of the tomb.

The group added their voices to her chant. All four dark-clad bodies swayed behind Odette.

Four. Liam jolted upright. There had been five just seconds ago. "Simone, do you know which one is missing?"

SHE OPENED her mouth to answer Liam just as the arm closed around her throat. It cut off her breath, dragging her back. Away from the voodoo ceremony. Away from Liam.

She thrashed, trying to break free. She opened her mouth to scream. But no sound came.

A knife blade pricked the tender skin below one ear. "I warned you to stay out of it," a voice hissed. "You should have listened. Now it's too late."

Pain sliced cold, cutting through the panic short-circuiting her mind. Something warm and sticky trickled down her neck. She struggled to concentrate. She'd gotten away before. She could do it again. Gathering her strength, she kicked backward. Her foot connected with a shin.

"Damn you!" The arm squeezed her throat. Something hard crashed against her skull.

Her thoughts reeled. Her mind went numb. She could feel her legs being dragged over rough ground, feel her body falling onto stone, the impact jarring her, but she couldn't do anything to prevent it. Her cheek rested on gravel. The smell wrapped around her like a wet blanket, clogging her throat, choking her.

The stench of death.

She fought to clear her thoughts, to make her mind function. A scraping sound caught her ear. The sound of stone on stone.

She reached out, her hand connecting with the carved stone wall of a sarcophagus. Forcing her eyes open, she raised her head. Walls surrounded her. Cold dank walls. Only a single sliver of moonlight marred the darkness. The sliver grew thinner.

She was in a crypt. And the door was closing.

Head pounding, Simone forced herself to her knees. She threw herself at the door, pushing with all her strength.

It sealed shut, plunging her into blackness.

Chapter Eight

Liam's heart slammed against his ribs. His labored breath roared in his ears. He'd been running for what seemed like hours, searching the crypts that towered on either side of the gravel road, combing the shadows for a shimmer of blond hair.

Cold dread seeped into him. He forced his feet to keep moving. Around a turn, down another long row of tombs. Ahead of him, the cemetery gate gaped like a screaming mouth. He looked up at the crypt that towered next to him. The black and red slashes on the unmarked tomb of Marie Laveau were stark in the moonlight.

Damn. He was back to the spot where they'd entered, and he still hadn't found any sign of Simone. He'd never find her in this maze. At least not until daybreak. And by then it might be too late.

It might already be too late.

He doubled over, head in hands. How could he have been so stupid? He should have kept Simone close beside him. He should have taken her hand when she'd offered it—taken it and never let it go.

But he hadn't taken her hand. He hadn't because he was afraid. Afraid of failing. Afraid of disappointing

her. Afraid of destroying her love the way his father
had destroyed his mother's.

"You aren't your father, Liam O'Reilly."

He spun around. There in the shadow of the adjacent
crypt, Odette LaFantary stared at him with dark eyes.
Her white robe and the white cloth wrapped around her
head glowed in the moonlight. "You are a different
generation. Your path will be different from his. You
will make it different."

For a moment he just looked at her, mind racing.
How had she known what he was thinking? Had he
spoken his thoughts out loud?

"You are searching for something."

"Simone." His fingers tightened around the grip of
his .22. He wanted to raise the gun, point it at the priestess and demand she tell him where Simone was. But
something told him he would get more answers from
her with questions than with threats. "Where is she?
What have you done with her?"

Odette raised a hand. "I don't know where she is.
And trust me, I haven't done anything with her."

"Why should I trust you?"

"You want my help. And what help I have to give
must be accepted in trust."

Could he take what she offered? Just a week ago he
wouldn't have considered it. A week ago he would have
written her off as a kook. But so much had happened.
So much had changed. "Simone trusts you. I guess I
can, too."

"And can you believe in the spirits? Because what I
have to tell you comes from them."

"I can try." For Simone, he'd try anything.

Odette nodded, the white head cloth bobbing in the
darkness. "Simone is with the snakes."

Liam cocked his head, not sure he'd heard her right. "Snakes?"

"Yes. You must give up control to the spirits and accept the heritage of your father to find her."

Liam shook his head. What she said didn't make sense. "Where are these snakes? What does my father have to do with any of this?"

Odette held out her hands in front of her, palms up. "That is all the *loa* have communicated to me. I don't know anything more. You must give control to the spirits. You must let go and believe."

Let go and believe. The same words Simone had said to him last night in the courtyard. He'd done it then. He had given up control and he had believed. In Simone. In himself. In magic.

Could he do it again?

His head spun. He leaned against the crypt and focused on the black and red markings to regain his bearings. When he looked back to Odette, the voodoo priestess was gone.

He rested his forehead against the stone of the crypt and closed his eyes. The stone was cool even in the warm and humid night and smelled of dust, of death, of life. He drew in a deep breath. He would do anything if it meant Simone's life was spared. Believe in anything. Accept anything. Risk anything. If she was returned to him, he'd never close himself off again.

Color mushroomed behind his closed eyelids. Purple, black and white. And in the swirls of color, he saw his father. A good father, a great cop, but a man with faults, with human frailties. Like himself. But not like him, either.

Different generations. Different paths.

He thought of Jordan. His younger brother had loved

Camille DuPree since he was a boy, and she loved him. Their love had lasted, even though they'd been apart for years. And it would last through whatever the future threw at them—even an unjust murder conviction. Maybe Liam was more like his brother than his father. Maybe the O'Reilly boys had both learned from the mistakes of their parents' marriage.

The image of his father came into sharper focus. On a chain around his neck hung the medallion he always wore. A medallion of Saint Patrick. And at the feet of the Irish saint, snakes twisted and writhed.

Snakes.

Liam pushed away from the crypt. Now that he knew what to look for, there was no time to waste.

But which way should he go?

Suddenly he knew. Turning back in the direction he came, he sprang into a run. His pulse hammered in his ears. His shoes thumped the hard-packed earth. He raked the top of each crypt and monument with his gaze as he passed. Finally he spotted Saint Patrick, a profusion of snakes curled at his feet.

He lunged for the crypt's door and slid the latch open. Fitting his fingers into a handle chiseled in the weathered granite, he yanked.

The door didn't budge.

He circled the small crypt. There had to be a way in. Why would the spirits bring him this far if there wasn't a way in? His foot hit something hard. He looked down. Metal glinted in the moonlight. A crowbar. The tool, no doubt, used to shut Simone inside the crypt in the first place. He picked it up and circled to the door. He fit the tool between the door and the wall, and pried the stone open.

Sitting on the floor of the crypt, Simone lifted her eyes to his.

He fell to his knees and gathered her into his arms. The salt of her tears stung his lips and mingled with the moisture from his own eyes. He held her for a long time, unable to let go. Finally he found the strength to speak. "You're safe."

"Thanks to you."

Thanks to Odette's spirits. He thought the words, but he didn't say them. He still wasn't sure what to believe as far as voodoo was concerned, but he *was* sure there was more to life than what met the eye.

Much more.

And he wanted to share all of it with Simone. But first, he needed to make things right. "About this morning…I need to explain."

She shook her head, her silky curls brushing his cheek. "All you need to do is hold me."

"No. You deserve more. And I want to give you more. I need to." He drew a breath. "Since I was seventeen, I believed maintaining control over my life was the key to happiness. If there was such a thing as happiness. It wasn't until the past few days that I realized I haven't really been living at all. You taught me that. You taught me about magic. About believing in something. You taught me to let go of past hurts and move on. You taught me so much, and what did I do? I pushed you away."

She pulled back from his shoulder. Her eyes glowed blue and sparkled with unshed tears. "It's okay, Liam. Really—"

He pressed a finger to her lips. "It's not okay. I said I couldn't think when I was around you. But the truth is, you make me think more clearly. When you're with me, I know what's truly important. I know what's possible in this life. And that's what scared me. I was afraid I'd fail you.''

She kissed the tip of his finger. "You could never fail me, Liam. I love you. With all my soul.''

"Enough to be my wife?" He held his breath. ''I know things have moved quickly between us. If you want more time—''

Her lips closed over his, cutting off his words, his thoughts. Her kiss was warm and generous and giving, and when she ended it, she looked deeply into his eyes. "I'd love to be your wife, Liam. And I don't need more time. I've been waiting my whole life for you. I've finally found where I belong. Right here in your arms.''

Liam pulled her tighter and kissed her. He belonged in her arms just as she belonged in his. Living. Loving. Believing.

Together forever.

ZACHARY

PATRICIA ROSEMOOR

Chapter One

First light stabbed ghostly fingers through the mausoleum-cast shadows at St. Louis Cemetery No. 1, and a hot wind carried with it the stench of death.

Having heard the call over his scanner, Officer Zachary Doucet made his unofficial arrival just behind the coroner and forensic team, but in time to see the crime-scene tape go up around Tony Fortune's body sprawled next to a now familiar gris-gris. Yet another of the voo-doo group dead. Zachary's gaze swept over the details, as if he could discern the identity of the murderer. Eyes open and staring, Fortune lay amidst the remains of burned-down candles and sacrifices to the voodoo gods. Though a deity needing a bottle of bourbon and a good cigar didn't make much sense to Zachary. Surely they had more lofty desires.

Maybe this time forensics would get lucky and secure a print off the bottle or saliva off the cigar tip. Yeah, sure they would…as if this killer was sloppy.

Still, criminals always missed something, and Zachary would give just about anything to be the one to break this case and get Jordan off. Thinking about the impossibility of doing so, he clenched his jaw. A uniform never got a crack at a homicide.

No, this was the purview of a task force headed up by Gary Yancy and Rebecca Romero. He spotted them to one side of the DeLyon crypt. Today Yancy was decked out in an embroidered vest below his canary-yellow jacket. Though Rebecca appeared controlled, Zachary knew she was angry. Her slim athletic body was so straight and stiff, she might have had a steel rod for a spine.

Letting his curiosity get the better of him, he circled around back and listened in.

"This proves Jordan O'Reilly isn't the voodoo killer," Becca was saying in a low heated voice.

Zachary got a glimpse of her. As she argued with her partner, her sun-kissed skin darkened a shade and her brown eyes deepened to black.

"How you figure that?" Yancy asked.

"He's behind bars," Becca said in that acerbic way of hers, "and if his voodoo is strong enough to get him out to kill Tony Fortune without anyone noticing, surely he would have simply disappeared or created a spell to misdirect us completely and saved himself a trial."

"Or his brother could've done a little sleight of hand."

Zachary stiffened and was about to step out and take on the nasty little man himself when Becca said, "You'd better explain yourself, Yancy."

"I wouldn't put it past Liam O'Reilly to manufacture evidence to prove his brother is innocent."

"Now you're calling *Liam* a murderer?"

"Blood tells."

"And what would you know about blood, Yancy?" Zachary asked as he slid into the open. "You got any in those veins?" Before a sputtering Yancy could answer, Zachary added, "Liam isn't one to manufacture anything and you know it."

"No, he can leave that to you!"

With that jab at Zachary's past, Yancy went to give orders to the forensic team.

Leaving a wide-eyed Becca staring at him.

Zachary stared back, appreciative as always of the contradiction that was Rebecca Romero, an exotic beauty in a plain paper wrapper. Lush dark-brown hair with red highlights was scraped back from an angular face and tucked into a French braid. Wide-spaced dark eyes and a full mouth went unadorned by makeup. Slender curves remained hidden beneath a loose pale-aqua shirt and pleated tan trousers. None of it mattered. He saw through her disguise.

Long fingers with short burgundy-polished nails worried the heavy gold cross hanging from a chain around her graceful neck. The same cross she'd worn all those years ago when she'd graduated from the Police Academy and been assigned as his partner, Zachary remembered. Her fingering the cross was a sure tell.

She was nervous.

Because of him.

He gave her a wry smile. "It's been a long time, Becca."

"Our paths don't cross much anymore," she admitted. "Well, not until this case."

They'd run into each other a couple of days before, after Liam had almost been run down by a car. He'd responded to the call, but the detectives had been right behind him.

Prior to that, he'd seen Becca around the station, but they hadn't come face-to-face on a case since she'd made detective. Before, really. Not since she'd turned against him for making certain a perp hadn't been able to get into his apartment and destroy evidence before the warrant arrived. Amazing tool, a little piece of twig. Jammed a lock good with a little effort. The small-time drug dealer had known he'd been made, though, and his lock tampered with. And when questioned, Rebecca had too quickly admitted what she'd seen her partner do.

Rebecca Romero was a sterling cop, a regular straight arrow in a city force that had enough corruption to make investigative reporters salivate for the next damning story. Zachary understood her motivation in telling the truth, though he didn't appreciate the results for himself. He hadn't made detective or even been promoted since the incident. And all he'd been doing was assuring them a collar of a hard-assed criminal.

Because of her, he might be wearing the same damn uniform for the rest of his natural life.

He couldn't help saying, "You do have trouble being on board with your partner."

"Wh-what?" Rebecca stammered.

Was Zach really going to bring up the past again? She took a step back. Which only prompted her ex-partner to take two steps forward, maneuvering so close to her that she imagined she could feel his breath on her face. His being so close tightened her chest and made her stomach knot.

"Fancy Yancy," he stated. "You don't agree that Jordan is a murderer...then again, you haven't spoken up in his behalf, either. Unusual for you, *chère*. So you've learned to play politics?"

She flushed at what she considered a criticism. "The evidence suggested Jordan did it. Until this." And despite her ethics, she wasn't so quick to jump on a fellow officer as she once had been.

"So what are you going to do?"

She swallowed hard. "I'm not sure yet."

"Then let's talk about it. About the murders," he clarified.

Rebecca took a big breath. "It's too early in the morning for me to have to deal with you, Zach. I haven't even had my first cup of coffee yet."

"So let's fix that."

She frowned. "I can't leave the scene to go to coffee with you."

"I wasn't suggesting you do. But you'll be wrapped up here soon and you're entitled to eat. You can meet me at Tante Lucille's for breakfast. You do remember the place, right?"

"I remember."

She remembered a lot of things, especially the way Zach used to make her heart beat faster when he smiled at her like that. The way her heart was beating faster now. She remembered the way she'd yearned to run her fingers through his spiked golden-brown hair. The way her breath sometimes caught in her throat when he stared at her, his heavy-lidded green eyes barely half-open, as if he had something personal in mind.

"Is it a date?" he asked, snapping her to.

"I thought it was just breakfast."

He grinned at her and backed off. "So you'll be there."

She took his measure. "Why, Zach? What's the big interest?"

She wanted him to say it. For a moment she thought he wouldn't.

His jaw worked and his lids lowered as if he could hide the truth from her. Then he looked straight at her, and the resemblance to the O'Reilly brothers hit her full force. They all had those same gorgeous eyes.

"No matter family differences, Jordan is my brother," Zach said. "And he's a good cop—like you. I won't let Yancy railroad him onto death row."

That was all she needed to hear. The words slipped over her tongue before she could stop herself. "Give me an hour, then. I'll meet you in an hour."

His smile broadened, popping the dimple in his right cheek. And then he turned and made tracks.

Rebecca stared at his retreating back. Her eyes dropped a little lower to where his uniform hugged a firm butt and steel-hard thighs, and she felt like fanning herself. Then she came to with a start.

What was wrong with her?

She was working a murder case and that was where her attention should be.

Groaning, she made her way back to Yancy, wondering how she was going to continue working with him when he was dead set on pinning the murder on the wrong man. On another cop. She was truly horrified that he seemed ready to accuse Liam of murder, as well, simply to protect his theory.

A theory that Zach apparently meant to blow out of the water.

Rebecca had seen Jordan talking with Zach more than once, and so understood why he would come through for the younger O'Reilly. Not so the middle brother. Considering the kind of snubs Liam had subjected him to over the years, she was amazed that Zach was ready to protect Liam, as well. Liam wouldn't even stay in the lounge for a coffee break if Zach came in.

There were all kinds of cops, as she'd come to know. Dedicated honest ones like Jordan and Liam. Ones like

Zach, ready to do anything to put a real criminal behind bars. Zach might have worked fast and loose at times, skirting the edge of proper procedure, but he'd always nailed the right man. And then there were the Yancys. Not many, thankfully, but even one cop willing to climb on the back of another to get promoted twisted her gut like nothing else.

So, no, she wasn't thrilled to be dealing with Zach again, but yes, she would show up at Tante Lucille's. She would put her own personal discomfort aside to save the life of a fellow officer. She could only hope that Zach had learned something since they'd worked together last. That he wouldn't think of going over that treacherous edge again, maybe taking her with him this time.

Rebecca knew the coming days wouldn't be easy for her if she agreed to work with Zach behind Yancy's back. She'd already ruined Zach's career, on top of sounding the death knell of their partnership. Too bad that hadn't been the end of her feelings for the man.

Working the crime scene took longer than she'd thought, but at last she was done. She could get away from the smell of death that permeated the cemetery in the growing morning heat and humidity. Rivulets of sweat ran down the center of her back and between her breasts, and even though her blouse was loose, it was already sticking to her.

"I need to run an errand," she told Yancy, "so I'll drop you off at the station and then meet you back there later." Fortunately she'd driven today.

"I can hook up with one of the uniforms and catch a ride," Yancy said, puffing up his slight chest and picking invisible lint from his canary-yellow jacket. "You go ahead."

The little peacock was being so agreeable that Rebecca said, "Great," and headed for her vehicle before he could change his mind.

No doubt he wanted to test his outrageous theory on someone else. At least she could take a break from her partner for a while, give herself a little time to think about what she could do to help Jordan.

She checked her watch. Nearly an hour and a half since Zach had left the cemetery grounds.

Would he have waited for her?

With both trepidation and a curl of excitement she didn't want to examine too closely, she started her car and headed for the neighborhood that bordered the French Quarter and a potential showdown that already had her nerves on edge.

Chapter Two

Zachary started on his third cup of Tante Lucille's coffee and stewed about the time, wondering if Becca was going to show up, after all.

He looked around the old Creole house that had been turned into a restaurant specializing in breakfast and lunch, each of its three small rooms turned into dining rooms. The place was homey and colorful, rather than fancy, with secondhand tables and chairs painted in decorative patterns. Lucille herself did all the cooking, and her Creole and Cajun food couldn't be beat. Her place was a well-kept secret with the locals. Just outside of tourist territory, it was often bursting at the seams.

But with the breakfast rush over, it was half-empty.

He checked his watch again, but willing Becca to show didn't seem to be working. She could have gotten caught up in the case. She could have changed her mind. He wouldn't blame her if she wanted nothing to do with him. When she'd ended their partnership, a big part of him had shut down, and he'd felt utterly alone. His mother was dead, at best he had a dicey relationship with his father, and his half brothers...well, at least Jordan was somewhat amenable, though Liam was another story, one he didn't trust.

But losing Becca's faith in him had been harder on him than anything. Harder than he'd wanted to admit.

The fresh-faced idealistic young cop had wangled her way into his system like no other woman had before or since. He'd counted on her, whether on the job or when he'd simply needed an ear to bend. He'd sought her approval and hadn't realized how much until it was too late. And he'd been so damned attracted to her he hadn't dated anyone else the whole year they were partners. Although he'd thought about making a move on Becca more times than he wanted to admit, he'd never done so *because* she'd been his partner. In his mind, a personal relationship might have gotten one of them killed.

Hearing the light metallic music made by the bells above the front door, he looked up to see her walking toward him, and a wave of bitterness and longing hit his gut. He'd been smart to keep his distance from Becca personally; otherwise her betrayal might have destroyed him.

She stopped at the opposite side of the table from him. He stared at her, his lids lowered so she couldn't read his thoughts.

"You made it," he said casually, as if he wasn't feeling a huge sense of relief.

"I said I would."

"Sit."

She sat.

He swept his hungry gaze over her as she took a sip of water and used her menu to fan herself. Stray hairs clung to her long neck, already wet with sweat. Her blouse was damp, too, a darker streak down the center clinging to her flesh and accentuating the lushness of her breasts. Before she could catch him staring, he averted his eyes to his menu, as if he hadn't had enough time to memorize the damn thing while waiting for her!

Becca turned over her cup, indicating she wanted coffee, then picked up her own menu. "Sorry I'm late," she murmured, sounding as if she was sorry for a whole lot more than a time glitch. "Thanks for waiting."

"Where would I go?" He sat back and stared at her openly. "You know I would wait for you forever, *chère.*"

She lifted an eyebrow and gave his uniform a once-over. "This detour isn't going to get you in hot water with Lieutenant Bennigan?"

"I called in," was all he said. Sometimes you had to get burned to see that justice was done, and he'd never been afraid of the heat.

Now that the morning traffic had slowed, Tante Lucille herself arrived at their table and filled Becca's cup with steaming chicory coffee. Ebony-skinned, dressed in a brightly patterned purple-and-orange caftan and her hair intricately braided with purple baubles, Lucille was a big woman, but she carried her size regally. Her face was always lit with good humor.

"Hey, babies, you ready to order now?" she asked with a smile that included them both.

Zachary winked at her. "You know what I want, Lucille, darlin'."

Laughing, the owner set the pot down on the table and took out her order pad. "Your usual, huh? Andoille hash with basted eggs and a corn muffin. And you, honey?"

Becca frowned as she continued to study the menu. "Ooh, the choices. A pecan waffle with a side of thick bacon, crabbie Benedict…"

"Which?"

"Both. And a side order of cheese grits and raisin toast with strawberry jam," Becca told her. "Oh, and fresh orange juice."

Though Lucille kept scribbling, she asked, "How many people you plannin' on feeding?"

"Just me."

"Becca always did have a healthy appetite." One of the many things Zachary remembered from their days working together.

Lucille took herself and her coffeepot into the kitchen, saying, "Wouldn't know it by the looks of her."

Indeed, Rebecca Romero was an amazing woman in many ways, Zachary thought.

As if compelled to explain, Becca said, "I missed breakfast and it's almost lunchtime. You know I don't believe in skipping meals."

"I like a woman with healthy appetites."

Her cheeks flushed and she cleared her throat and fingered her gold cross, but still, she didn't miss a beat. "We ought to get right down to business, don't you think?"

Zachary thought of turning that request back on her somehow just to see her squirm, but then he thought again. Their purpose here was serious—he meant to discuss the case with her. Besides which, he was still angry with Becca and he had to remember that. He needed to focus.

"So what does Fancy Yancy have against Jordan?" he asked, watching her add cream to her coffee.

"Nothing that I know of."

"Could've fooled me."

"Jordan was simply the easy suspect."

"I wonder if there isn't more to it."

Becca shrugged. ''Yancy doesn't exactly confide in me, you realize. But I know he doesn't like your father. Something about a lost promotion before your father retired from the force. You'd think Yancy would be over it by now, but maybe he's taking his hatred for your father out on his kids. All I know for sure is, he's building a case he can get promoted on.''

''Over another cop's body.''

''That's the worst of it,'' she said.

At least they agreed about something. Zachary couldn't tolerate a cop using another's back to climb to the top any more than she could. And the cop whose back was being stomped over happened to be his blood kin, no matter that his own name wasn't O'Reilly.

He asked, ''What's your take on the real murderer, then?''

She didn't hesitate. ''One of Odette's followers.''

''Any guesses which one?''

''Not yet, but there aren't many left, are there? The field's been narrowed down to three. The amorous widow, Miss Lulu, the not-so-grieving sister, Helen Gaylord, and the financially stricken spinster, Lisa Cantro.''

Zachary's mind was going in a very different direction—to the voodoo priestess, rather than to one of her followers. ''What about Odette LaFantary herself?''

''No!''

''You sound awfully sure of that.''

''I just know her, that's all. Odette may be ambitious and may rely a little heavily on showmanship to make a living, but neither of those facts make her a murderer.''

''You know her personally?''

''Since we were kids. Her dad was a handyman. After

my father died, he did some work around our place, and Odette used to keep him company when she wasn't in school. She and I hit it off from the first.''

Zachary knew Becca's father had been a cop like his, and that she'd joined the force to make him proud. The same way he had, he guessed, something else they had in common. Neither of them had gotten that approval they'd sought, but at least her father had an excuse. He'd been killed on the job when she was a kid. Things she'd shared with him when they were partners came back in a rush.

Shifting uncomfortably in his seat, he asked, ''So you and Odette are friends now?''

''Well, we don't see each other on a regular basis, but I go into her shop and, sure, I still consider her a friend.''

''Then maybe you're too close. Maybe you should back up and rethink her involvement in this case. Maybe you simply don't see what you don't want to see.''

Becca gaped at him for a moment, then snapped, ''That's not me, Zach!''

Her response hit him like a slap and he knew she spoke the truth. ''No, it isn't, is it.''

How could he have forgotten she didn't ignore anything, not even when it meant destroying her partner's career? Integrity was everything to Becca.

Luckily their food came, giving him some time to regroup. They ate in silence for a while. Becca's appetite seemed diminished. She barely tasted the various dishes before pushing her many plates away.

''You're going to disappoint Lucille.''

Ignoring his observation, she said, ''So I get the not-wanting-another-cop-to-go-down part, but what about the brother part? When did you and Jordan get close?''

''We're not close. We're on neutral ground. We're trying to relate, have some kind of friendly relationship. If Liam didn't keep getting in the way…''

''You always had a major problem with him.''

''Uh, not really—Liam's the one with issues.'' Probably because Liam had thought he was his father's first-born until at seventeen he'd been introduced to his older-by-less-than-a-year half brother.

''Oh, right. The great Zachary Doucet never has issues. He's too chill. It doesn't bother him at all that his father was stepping out with his mother while he was engaged to another woman.''

''Yeah, he was a real man's man,'' Zachary said, unable to keep the irony from his tone.

He'd told his father what he'd thought of him, and the words hadn't been uttered with admiration. Becca was right about him, though. He *did* have issues. He was the firstborn and he was the only son barely acknowledged. Liam and Jordan had only known about him for a decade or so. He'd known about his father's legitimate family ever since he could remember.

''Have you ever tried with Liam?''

He blinked and Becca came back in focus. ''With Liam?'' He shook his head. ''You know how it was, still is…well, was until the other day.''

''What happened the other day?''

''He asked for my help in proving Jordan innocent.''

''That's big. Very big.''

''Liam loves *Jordan* like the brother he is and would do anything for him, even ask *me* for help.'' Liam had even admitted Zachary was his brother to Jordan's lawyer, Simone Jones. As far as he knew, that was a first.

Becca reached across the table. "It's a start, Zach. Take it and run with it."

"Why should I?"

"Because it's what you've always wanted." She took a big breath and asked, "What is it you want from *me?*"

Truth be told, he wanted everything from her, he thought, feeling the old attraction growing. Her hand on his made him yearn for all the things he'd never had that he wanted, and she'd topped the list. But that was then and this was now.

He slipped his hand from hers, picked up his cup and took a sip of coffee to distract himself from his thoughts.

"I want to find the real murderer, which means taking a closer look at the survivors in the voodoo group. Perhaps we need to pay Miss Lulu a visit. Liam saw her with Tony Fortune and wondered whether they were having an affair while Spiro was still alive," he said, once more reminded that he'd been the product of an unfaithful relationship. "Cheating on your spouse... getting caught..."

"Great motive for murder," she finished for him.

Chapter Three

Rebecca pulled up and parked at the curb in front of Miss Lulu's Garden District mansion, where she was to meet Zach, as agreed that morning. Having come straight from the police station, where she'd had to put up with more of Yancy than she could stand, she only hoped Zach wouldn't give her a hard time about anything.

Once this case was concluded, she resolved to ask for a new partner, provided Yancy didn't get promoted right out of the detective squad for doing such a good job of ruining Jordan and maybe Liam, too. But no, surely she and Zach could turn things around for Jordan.

The sun had already set and shadows cast across the mansion's front deepened the lavender paint to mauve. The property was surrounded by a lacy wrought-iron fence similar to that guarding the second-floor balcony. Getting out of her car, she took a good look around. A side yard had been turned into one of the flourishing gardens for which the area had been named, and a smaller building in a similar design and color backed the lush property.

As the fragrance of gardenias enveloped her, a movement caught her eye, and she wondered if it was simply coincidence or if someone was watching her. Rebecca stared into the gloom. Nothing. And then a car turned the corner and stopped, diverting her attention. The vehicle parked at the curb and Zach got out.

As he joined her, she quickly registered his street clothes. They looked as if they were made for his body—pale-gray trousers and a darker silk T-shirt that revealed the musculature in his shoulders and arms and hinted at a six-pack abdomen.

Irritated with herself for noticing, she said, "You changed clothes. Is that to make Miss Lulu think you're part of the detective division?"

His open expression closed. "I never pretend to be what I'm not. I thought a shower and change of clothing was in order. I'm off duty, so I can wear whatever I want."

He leaned past her to open the front gate, which was embellished with the DeLyon *D* and *L,* and in doing so, brushed her arm with his. Beneath her blouse, her skin pebbled, and Rebecca felt herself flush. Hoping to hide it, she tuned and started down the walk. Aware of Zach close behind her, she took a deep breath and steadied herself before climbing the two steps to the porch and ringing the doorbell.

A young woman in a maid's uniform answered. "I'm sorry, but Miss Lulu is not receiving visitors this evening."

"She'll want to talk to us," Zach assured her, his voice low and honey-sweet.

Trying to ignore the thrill bubbling through her, Rebecca showed the woman her badge. "We need to talk to Mrs. DeLyon about the murders."

Eyes widening, the maid bobbed her head and let them in. Then to one side of the foyer, a two-story space crowned by an elaborate crystal chandelier, she picked up a phone that apparently served as an intercom.

Although the maid spoke quietly, Rebecca heard the words *police* and *murder*.

Dropping the receiver back into its cradle, the young woman said, "Miss Lulu will be with you directly," before disappearing down a hallway.

Zach waited until she was out of sight before saying softly, "So why do you think Miss Lulu is playing the recluse today?"

"Maybe she's more upset by Fortune's death than she was by her husband's."

Before they could continue their speculation, the sound of high-heeled shoes on the stairs above reached their ears, and Rebecca glanced up to see Miss Lulu make her entrance. The not-so-grieving widow wore a simple black sheath tonight. Her red hair was slicked back from her face. And she carried a lace-trimmed handkerchief in a bejeweled hand. As she descended, she glanced from Rebecca to Zach, and her eyes suddenly gleamed with interest as brightly as did the diamonds in her rings and bracelet.

"Oh, someone new. Have they replaced that nice Detective Yancy on the case?"

"No, not at all," Rebecca told her. "I simply wanted to speak to you myself. This is Officer Zachary Doucet. He kindly agreed to accompany me."

Miss Lulu tilted her head and, if Rebecca wasn't mistaken, batted her fake eyelashes at Zach.

"Officer Doucet, so nice to meet you," Miss Lulu said, moving forward and tucking a proprietary hand under his arm. "Let's step into the front parlor, shall we? May I ring for some refreshments?"

"Not for me, thanks," Zach said.

Rebecca said nothing, but apparently Miss Lulu's offer didn't extend to her.

Once they made themselves comfortable, with Miss Lulu ensconced in a chair facing Zach and her, Rebecca said, "You do know about Tony Fortune, right?"

Miss Lulu tried to hide her expression by dropping her face into the hand holding her handkerchief, but the gesture was a sure sign that she was nervous.

"Yes, I did hear that poor Tony became the latest victim of the Voodoo Killer." She bit her lip and her eyes watered a bit. She dabbed at them. "Tony was such a dear friend of Spiro's and mine. I am surrounded by tragedy," she said bravely, her lower lip quivering.

Great acting, Rebecca thought as she asked, "Since Tony Fortune was such a dear friend and all, do you know if he had any enemies?"

"Enemies? Tony?"

"Right. The kind who might have wanted to see him dead."

"You think *I* know who had it in for him?" Miss Lulu appeared shocked. "No, of course not. I don't know who killed Tony any more than I know who killed my Spiro. Or poor Sadie. Of course I don't know anything about these terrible murders, except…Odette promised to have a ceremony to find the one responsible before anyone else dies."

Zachary stared at Becca. Though she raised her eyebrows, he figured she wasn't going to ask questions where her old friend was concerned.

She surprised him.

"Do you really believe Odette LaFantary is truly that powerful?".

"Well, yes, of course she is!"

''Then it's a shame she hasn't discerned the real murderer yet.''

''I...I don't think voodoo works that way.''

''How *does* it work?'' Becca pressed. ''Can it *kill?*''

Color rose in Miss Lulu's cheeks and she lost that innocent, slightly bewildered expression. Zach figured she'd had enough. But before she could dismiss them, he reached over, took her hand and smiled at her.

''These murders have been a terrible thing for all involved, but an especially hard burden on a gentle soul such as yourself. I'm glad to see that your late husband made certain to provide for you.'' He indicated their surroundings. ''It must give you great peace of mind.''

She smiled sadly and murmured, ''Yes, thankfully.''

He glanced past her to the photographs displayed. There were several of Miss Lulu and DeLyon together and, definitely separated from these, several youngish adults.

Figuring that these young adults had nothing to do with Miss Lulu, he went fishing. ''What about your husband's children by his first marriage? Hopefully, your stepchildren won't try to take away your beautiful home.''

''They could never do that,'' she replied. ''My dear smart Spiro made sure everything was in both our names just last year, so that if anything happened to him...''

As if remembering she should be more upset since something had indeed happened to him, she blinked rapidly and used the lacy hanky to wipe away nonexistent tears. Zach exchanged a look with Becca, who simply appeared unimpressed.

''You'll have to forgive me,'' the widow said with a

catch in her voice. "It's been such a traumatic time for me."

"I'll just bet," Becca said.

Obviously Miss Lulu didn't miss the acerbic tone, for the woman straightened her spine and sniffed. "I'm so worn-out by the recent tragic events that I feel the need for a lie-down and a cool compress."

A dismissal if ever he'd heard one.

A few minutes later, he and Becca had taken their leave and were out on the sidewalk.

"Am I kidding myself or do I see a motive here?" she asked, turning to gaze at the house.

Zach studied her profile, softened in the low light, and his chest tightened. "Money is always a potential motive, doubly so when the spouse in question is ready to wander. I wouldn't be shocked if we learn Miss Lulu prompted DeLyon to make those changes in his holdings and then arranged for his death. I'll suggest Liam look into that angle. He can talk to DeLyon's grown kids and get their take on it."

Becca nodded and met his gaze. "Fortune could have been a willing accomplice…but maybe Miss Lulu got rid of him because he was the only person who could talk."

The exchange reminded him of the great team they'd made when they'd worked together before. They'd been able to anticipate each other, like two parts of a whole. He'd never felt that sense of completion with anyone else.

"Interesting theory," he said. "But what about Sadie Marceau? Why kill her?"

"She found out somehow. Maybe she overheard Miss Lulu and Fortune talking about it."

"Now all we have to do is prove it, *chère*."

"You get Liam on DeLyon's kids, and I'll think about our next move."

Becca certainly had taken charge, Zachary thought as he watched her cross to her car. He wasn't sure how he felt about that. He kind of liked it when she'd been young and green and had needed him.

Professionally, anyway.

REBECCA HAD JUST STARTED her car when she looked across to the DeLyon property and saw furtive movement in the shadows by the smaller building in back.

Someone was there! She'd known it before, but she'd been distracted by Zach's arrival.

She cut her engine, but before she could signal him, Zach pulled his car away from the curb and was gone with a screech of tires. She grabbed her flashlight and quietly climbed out, intending to see what was going on.

What if they'd been wrong about Miss Lulu? What if *she* was about to receive a gris-gris? What if the murderer was ready to strike again?

The gate opened with a scrape and Rebecca slipped back onto the property. Rounding the corner, she heard a noise and was certain it came from the smaller building. Staying close to the side of the house, she drew her gun and tiptoed through the garden.

Her heart began to pound the way it had when she was a rookie and tracking criminals on foot, something she hadn't done for years, at least not alone.

Not in the dark.

Not after a killer.

Stopping at the back corner of the house, she stared toward the smaller building and listened hard. Nothing. She hadn't imagined seeing someone, though. Her mouth was dry. She began to advance one slow, careful step at a time.

Suddenly she was there at the open doorway of the outbuilding, her moment of reckoning. Gripping her gun with one hand, she snapped on her flashlight with the other and lit the interior with the harsh magnesium glow.

Garden tools shone back at her.

No one was inside, but a strong smell of gasoline made her gasp. Then she heard it. A footfall. Heart hammering, she started to turn…

Too late!

Her head jerked as something solid made contact with her skull. Her hands went limp, and weapon and flashlight hit the ground as she staggered forward. Two hands shoved her hard in the middle of her back.

She stumbled and went down to her knees.

Crack!

This time her head exploded into pinpricks of light and she pitched facedown to the ground. The dark place beckoned as she heard an ominous scratch and a hiss….

Chapter Four

That Becca's headlights hadn't appeared behind him as he pulled out knotted Zachary's gut with worry. He drove around the block. Her car was still there. She wasn't.

Where the hell was she? He couldn't see her from his vehicle, so he parked once more and set out to find her. Instincts telling him something was wrong, he circled the DeLyon house only to see flames shoot up from a small building around back.

Moving faster, he yelled, "Becca!"

Thinking fast, he found a garden hose and turned it on full blast, then advanced while spraying the burning building with water. As he drew closer to the open doorway, smoke billowed out at him, stinging his eyes.

Squinting, he could make out something on the floor…legs…a body…

"Becca!" Frantic, he doused water over her as a precaution. "Can you hear me?"

She didn't answer. Didn't make a sound.

Didn't move.

Chest tight, Zachary aimed the blast of water at flames that were creeping too close to Becca's inert form. He held his breath as he moved in to get her. But she lay so still that he feared the smoke had gotten to her already. Even as he doused the last of the flames into oblivion, he hooked his free hand in the waistband of her trousers and dragged her out of the building. Then he tossed the hose and dropped to the ground next to her.

Was she even breathing?

Rivulets of water from her wet hair streamed down her forehead and over her cheeks as he positioned her flat on her back. When he put a hand behind her neck and pulled up so that he could check her airway, her mouth fell open. He settled his face closer to hers. A slight breath against his skin assured Zachary that she was alive.

"Becca, wake up," he said, rocking her shoulder gently when he really wanted to shake her awake.

Suddenly Becca gasped and her eyes flashed open. "Zach," she whispered, tone and expression making him think she was glad to see him. "Thank God it's you."

Zachary felt exactly the same way.

Before he could think it through, he gently brushed his mouth over hers in a physical expression of relief. As their lips met, hers opened slightly. An invitation…one he couldn't resist.

Slipping an arm under her back, he lifted Becca so that they were sitting face-to-face and chest-to-chest. She shifted and slid her arms up around his neck, and this time when their lips met, so did their worlds.

And his imploded.

Forgetting everything but the woman in his arms, Zachary kissed her sweetly, deeply, the way he'd always dreamed of doing.

For he had dreamed of having Rebecca Romero in

his arms, in his bed, more times than he wanted to admit. His pulse was humming, his blood flowing fast, his heart beating like a drum, a sound that echoed through his head.

He needed her so, and Becca clung to him as if he were her life force.

He didn't know how long they remained, bodies and lips locked together, but the wetness of her clothing finally penetrated his and made him come to his senses. As painful as it was, he pulled away.

What had he been thinking?

Even now her attacker might be watching for a chance to finish the job.

He listened hard and cast his gaze around the grounds, but heard nothing and saw no movement, not even from the house. No one seemed to have noticed what had happened out here.

Sounding embarrassed, Becca mumbled, "My gun. I dropped it in the shed."

"I'll get it."

"My flashlight, too."

Seconds later, he handed her both items. "How'd this fire get started, anyway? Why were you here?"

"I saw movement toward the rear of the building and came to investigate."

"Without backup?"

She ignored that. "I smelled gasoline and then someone hit me." She rubbed a spot on the back of her head. "Maybe we'd better call this in."

"Right."

As Zachary pulled out his radio, she started to get to her feet. He grabbed hold of her arm to stop her.

"Hey, stay put. Just wait for the paramedics."

"I'm fine."

"Indulge me."

"I don't need paramedics."

"You're getting them, anyway. You could have a concussion. How does your head feel?"

"Hurts."

"I'll bet."

So while he called in, she sat there quietly, turned on her flashlight and swept the beam over the grounds. She saw no sign of whoever had mugged her. But she did notice a peculiar lump on the ground nearby. The moment he was off the radio, she pointed it out to him.

"I see it." Taking the light from her, he moved to inspect the thing more closely. A dark wad of feathers. "Yep, one of those voodoo charms like DeLyon and Sadie got."

"And Tony Fortune."

"We'll have to warn Miss Lulu."

"If it was meant for her," Becca said.

"What do you mean?"

The way she was looking at him made his blood run cold.

"What if it was meant for me?" she whispered.

Her words cut through him, making him feel crazed that Becca could now be targeted for death.

REBECCA FELT crazed for having given in to her feelings for Zach.

What had she been thinking, kissing him like that?

The authorities arrived so quickly that she didn't have time to cave in to her embarrassment. The next hour was filled with a cacophony of questions, from the uniform who took the report, from the crime-scene investigator and paramedics, and, once the household was alerted, from Miss Lulu herself.

As Rebecca's blood pressure was checked for the third time, Miss Lulu wailed, "The Voodoo Killer is after *me* now!" and Becca's stomach clutched.

One of the officers escorted the widow back to the house, saying, "Maybe you ought to call someone to stay the night with you, ma'am."

"I demand police protection!"

At least Yancy hadn't shown up, Rebecca thought, thankful for small favors. Somehow, she got through it all, no thanks to Zach who hovered over her and made her nerves stretch taut.

"Detective Romero should go to the hospital, right?" he asked the paramedic.

Rebecca said, "No hospital."

"You're not the medical professional." Zach turned to the young man who was packing up. "What about it?"

"There's no sign of concussion. She can go home but shouldn't drive. And someone should wake her every hour or so, just to check on her."

"But you don't have anyone at home," Zach said to Rebecca.

"I'll find someone," she replied, and when he didn't argue, she should have been forewarned.

He barely waited until the ambulance door swung closed. "You can leave your car here until morning. I'll take you home."

"Whoa—"

Before she could finish her objection, he said, "Give me an alternative. Who do you want to alarm about the situation? Your mom? Your sister?"

"A friend."

He pulled out a cell phone. "Give me a name and number."

Because Rebecca didn't want to involve any of her friends in this mess, either, she gave in. "All right." Zach was giving her the easiest solution to the problem. "I'll let you take me home."

A promise she was sure to regret.

Only she didn't realize how much until a quarter of an hour later when they ended up at the Canal Street dock in line for the car ferry. Realizing where he meant to take her, she tensed.

"Um, I live on this side of the Mississippi," she said.

"I'm well aware of that."

"I thought you were taking me home."

"I am. To mine. Algiers Point."

For once in her life, she was speechless. Freaked out and trying not to show it, she decided that this was one time when silence was golden. Zach was taking her over and there wasn't a lot she could do about it. In truth, not a lot she *wanted* to do at the moment.

"How are you feeling, *chère?*"

"A little tired," she admitted.

"We can just sit in the car and relax," Zach said as he drove onto the ferry. "Close your eyes and rest. I'll watch over you."

What she wouldn't admit, at least not to him, was that she was afraid.

Fear was something she'd grown used to over the years. No matter how well trained she was, as a cop she never knew when a suspect might turn on her and hurt her in a struggle to get free—which was how her father had died. But that was a different kind of fear. She was able to sublimate it, because it wasn't personal. This was. Whether or not she had been the original intended victim, someone had tried to kill *her*. Lighting that match had gone beyond the person's need for self-preservation. He or she could simply have run and gotten away.

Suddenly it seemed inevitable that the Voodoo Killer would go after her again.

Shivering, she wrapped her arms around herself as if she could contain her fright, not let Zach notice it. He'd always said he could smell fear in a suspect from a mile away, so why not in her? Or maybe he already had and that was why he was being so kind, insisting on taking care of her.

Not liking the notion, she shifted uneasily.

She wanted more than Zach's kindness. She wanted his respect. She also wanted him to hold her, to kiss her, to—

The blow to her head might have made her vulnerable, but she would be in her right mind in the morning, Rebecca hoped.

"Rest well, *chère,*" Zach murmured, lightly caressing her cheek.

Refusing to open her eyes and look at him, Rebecca swallowed hard. Though he really *was* being kind, her mind betrayed her. She couldn't stop the memories from haunting her—the way she'd hungered after him and especially the way their partnership had ended....

Chapter Five

The ferry ride was over too quickly for Rebecca's comfort. They would be alone all too soon. As they whipped down the street in his car, she stared out the window.

The Algiers Point neighborhood was foreign to her; she'd been on this side of the Mississippi in the city itself only a couple of times. Which was nothing unusual, considering some Algiers residents had spent their whole lives on this side of the river, never venturing across to the French Quarter or downtown. But then the river became a memory as she and Zachary drove along a street with shotgun houses lining both sides. On the next block, Victorians and Greek revivals were wedged between smaller houses with gingerbread trim. Zach slowed the car and parked in front of a Creole cottage.

The place where she would spend the night.

With him.

Part of her wanted to flee from both—the past stood between her and Zach and probably always would—while another part of her longed to be privy to his private life. But although he was treating her to his soft side for the moment, Rebecca knew he would never forget her betrayal, would never forgive her.

Zach opened the car door and held out his hand. Reluctantly she gave him hers. At first touch, a thrill shot through her.

"Careful." Zach helped her out. And when she tried to rush by him, he held her fast, saying, "No need to hurry in the Big Easy, *chère*."

"No need to worry, either."

"You don't have to prove anything to me," he said.

She attributed her confusion to the lump on her head. She let Zach help her up the steps to the porch, but then, as she waited for him to unlock the door, her mouth went dry and her pulse sped up. They'd never been together like this before, and she didn't know what to expect. He held open the door and, when she stepped in, snapped on a ceiling fan that moved the thick air around.

"Sorry I didn't leave on the air conditioner." He moved to a window unit and turned it on. "It'll take a while for the place to cool down."

She nodded and took in her surroundings. The cottage charmed her. The living area glowed with burnished gold walls and polished antique pieces that dressed up the plainer contemporary couch and chairs.

Zach came right up behind her, so close she could feel his heat. "Do you want to go to bed right away," he asked, his breath teasing her ear, the suggestion in his words thrilling her to the core, "or would you like something cool to drink first? Iced tea?"

A vision of them in bed together made her breath come out in a rush. "Tea, please."

"You'll want to get out of the wet clothes."

Indeed, the humidity had kept her shirt and trousers clinging damply to her skin. But the idea of removing them, of putting on his shirt or robe, instead, felt too intimate. Too intimidating.

"They'll dry."

"Suit yourself." He brushed past her and headed for the doorway that led to the kitchen and the promised iced tea. "I just don't want you to be uncomfortable."

Why, then, did he keep seeming to come on to her? she wanted to ask, but bit her tongue, instead. Something had happened on the DeLyon estate that transcended old hurts. Zach was attracted to her, maybe even cared for her as much as she did him. For the moment, at least, he seemed to have tucked away any negative feelings.

So what was she going to do about it?

That was the question uppermost on her mind as she prowled the room seeking a distraction, something to take her mind off this unexpected development.

She was drawn to the far wall, which was covered with photographs of people who looked vaguely like Zach. His mother's side of the family, she assumed. But then she came to a photograph that made her stare—a man and his two boys, a young Liam and Jordan. In the past, Zach had let slip bits and pieces of his disappointments with them, but he'd never opened up to her fully.

Hearing his tread behind her, she turned to face him. He handed her a tall glass of iced tea. Grateful, she took a long sip before commenting on the photograph.

"Do Liam and Jordan know your father gave you this photograph of them?"

He shrugged. "Actually he didn't give it to me. And if they knew, I wouldn't care what they thought about it."

A lie, Rebecca decided, hearing the old wound in his

voice. "If your father didn't give you the photo, then who did?"

"I took it myself. When I was a kid, I used to play spy…I used to pretend…"

When he faltered, she finished for him, "That you were part of the O'Reilly family?"

"Family is important to me, Becca, and whether or not Liam ever accepts it, we have the same blood running through our veins."

"Maybe he'll come around."

"Don't count on it. He's only speaking to me now for Jordan's sake."

"But your helping Jordan has to mean something to him. To all of them," she added, thinking of their father.

"Ironic if it takes something like this happening to one of his other sons for me to get the old man's notice." Zach shook his head. "From the time I was a kid, I've tried to make him proud of me."

"I'm sure you have."

"If that's true, he's never let me know it."

"A lot of parents are like that."

"Do a lot of parents refuse to recognize their own kid?"

"Oh, come on, Zach—"

"I'm serious. I'm our father's firstborn, but you'd never know it. For all the time he's spent in my company, you wouldn't know we're related at all. He played fast and loose with my mother and then with me. He betrayed us both."

Rebecca didn't know what to say to make him feel better. Owen O'Reilly should be ashamed of himself, not because he'd sired Zach, but because he'd made his son feel as if he'd come up short, as if he was unworthy, as if he was less than he was.

Less of a son, less of a brother, less of a cop, less of a man.

Knowing that attitude had to have affected Zach, she impulsively placed a hand on his arm. He covered her fingers with his, and she felt an odd connection with him. At last she understood why he played fast and loose with suspects, why he'd taken her corroborating that accusation against him so hard, why her honesty had set him against her so bitterly at the time.

Betrayed by his father, by his brother Liam, by his partner. Always betrayed by the people who meant the most to him.

But the way Zach was looking at her now was not at all condemning.

"As I see it," he told her, "blood is more powerful than anything. Except maybe love."

Rebecca's heart pounded and she felt the last of her barriers melt. She'd never felt so close to Zach. They'd shared so much in the past. She wanted to share more.

Setting down her tea, she moved closer. She'd always wanted to touch that rough-hewn face, wanted to see his expression change from surprise to understanding to desire, as it did now while she trailed her fingertips along his jawline. He caught her hand and without taking his gaze from hers, kissed her palm, nipped at the fleshy pad of a forefinger, then drew it into his mouth.

Rebecca gasped. Despite the coolness of the air coming from the window unit, heat seared her. She was no fool. She knew what was happening here between them. Making her dreams come true if only for the night—a night that would make her feel alive and safe and bulletproof—was in her grasp.

Seizing the opportunity before it slipped away, she murmured, ''You were right about my clothes. They are wet and uncomfortable. So why don't you take them off?''

He lowered his eyelids to half-mast, but she could still see his irises, a mesmerizing green in the dim light. His features grew as taut as her breasts suddenly felt.

''That knock on the head is affecting you, making you talk nonsense.''

Longing for his intimate touch, she said, ''Maybe the injury is affecting me, but not in the way you mean. It took a brush with death to make me realize how short life is, how much time we waste not asking for what we want.''

She moved into Zach and this time asked him with her lips. Groaning, he caught her to him and made her feel as if she were drowning in that kiss.

Suddenly her head was whirling, *she* was whirling, and he was dancing her back against the wall. He pinned her there with his lips, his hands too busy seeing to her request. He unbuttoned her blouse, unzipped her trousers, removing first her clothing, then his own.

His kisses traveled along her jaw and down her neck. He caught a nipple with his teeth, then drew it into his mouth. The sensation was so sweet that a sound of pleasure caught at the back of her throat. But that small pleasure was easily surpassed when he explored lower and lower still and tongued the hot wet flesh between her thighs.

Her hips pushed at him as she tossed her head to one side and pressed her shoulders back into the wall. He opened her wider, hooking one arm under a thigh and lifting. Her other leg trembled so, that without support behind her, she would have fallen.

He brought her to the brink and then abandoned her center. He was traveling upward with more kisses—belly, navel, breasts, mouth.

He shifted slightly and she felt his hard tip pressing against her center. He paused there, as if awaiting permission to enter. Opening herself to him, she pulled him inside.

She clung to him then, arms around his neck, so that when he dipped and hooked her other thigh and rose with her, she was steady. Her legs fit around his hips like parts of a puzzle. He held her against the wall with his body, sending his hands in search of hers. His fingers circled her wrists, and then he tugged upward and pinned them against the wall just above her head.

His kiss was hard and deep, his tongue moving with the same speed as his hips, darting in and out in the same seductive rhythm. One of his hands now held both of hers while the other dipped between their bodies. The moment he touched her, she hit the edge, but she kept moving and the sensation kept growing until she couldn't take any more.

Wave after wave of pleasure rocked her world, and she cried out, only to hear Zach's echoing bellow as he, too, came. Hands freed, she draped herself around his shuddering body and clung to him as if she would never let go.

Chapter Six

Rebecca fought her way into a state of wakefulness and immediately regretted it when she found herself surrounded by mosquito netting...and by Zach. His arm lay possessively across her middle.

Aghast, she remembered how she'd wound up in his bed, how he'd wakened her every hour as instructed to make sure she was all right.

She'd been all right, all night long, thanks to him.

But now, the cold light of morning brought with it some common sense.

Had she lost her mind, sleeping with Zachary Doucet?

Carefully slipping out of bed so as not to wake him, she threw on her clothes in the living room and tiptoed to the front door. There she hesitated. Should she wake him, tell her she was leaving? What if he wouldn't let her leave, if he seduced her and took her back into his bed?

Weak-kneed at the thought, she made her escape. She needed alone time. Time to think things through. They'd always had different styles of doing things, and she wasn't sure she could reconcile herself to accepting his. On foot, she hurried back the way they had driven the night before. When she got within sight of the river, she spotted a cruising taxi and flagged it down.

Intending to get her car, she mumbled, ''Garden District,'' and tried to relax against the back seat.

Knowing Yancy had the day off, Rebecca decided to follow up on some things while he was gone. Things she was certain Zach would like to be privy to. But she didn't want to wait until he was off duty that night. No, to be honest, that wasn't the problem. She wasn't sure she wanted to spend more time in his company at all until she had things figured out.

Once home, she quickly showered and washed her hair, all the while realizing she was listening for the phone. It didn't ring. Could Zach still be sleeping? Remembering the exercise they'd both had throughout the night, she figured he probably was. Part of her was relieved; another part of her was strangely annoyed that she'd left his bed and he hadn't even noticed.

After eating a quick breakfast, she checked in at the station, then headed for Odette's shop. Taboo was in a busy part of the French Quarter, and the tourists were out in droves today, but the place was empty when she entered.

Dressed in a loose purple-and-teal caftan, tiny braids wound around her head in an intricate pattern, the priestess herself sat behind the cosmetics counter. At the bell's tinkling, she looked up from the large leatherbound book she was reading and immediately set it out of sight.

Her old childhood friend didn't seem especially glad to see her, Rebecca thought. Odette's expression was aloof, even suspicious.

''What can I do for you, Rebecca?''

No niceties, so no point in evasions. ''The truth.''

"Which truth would that be?"

"The Voodoo Killer. You know Jordan O'Reilly is innocent as well as I do. Tony Fortune's death proves it."

"Yes. But why hasn't Jordan been released?"

"A formality," Rebecca lied, knowing it would take another viable suspect to trump Yancy. "What about your regulars? How well do you know them? Do you think one of them could be the murderer?"

Movement caught Rebecca's attention, and she glanced toward the rear of the store, a throbbing red-and-gold cave devoted to voodoo. Marie Germain busied herself there, setting product in a glass case. But Rebecca was certain Odette's new assistant was eavesdropping—she couldn't miss the disapproving expression on the woman's face.

"You expect a lot from me, Rebecca," Odette said.

"I can't imagine you want to see anyone else die. I've never suspected you," she added, just in case her old friend had the wrong idea.

Nodding, Odette pulled out a deck of Tarot cards and indicated that Rebecca should cut it.

Unsure of how much she believed in any hoodoo or voodoo practiced by her friend, she hesitated. "You think you'll find the answer in that deck? If so, then we detectives are wasting our time running around and investigating when we could simply have a Tarot reader give us our answers."

Odette's smile was knowing. "Not all Tarot readers interpret the cards with my skill." She waited for Rebecca to make the next move.

Clenching her jaw, Rebecca cut the deck, after which the self-styled voodoo priestess began laying out a six-card pattern on the counter.

"The Voodoo Killer was born in the descent from light to darkness," Odette intoned.

Rebecca gazed at the cards—the Hanged Man, the five of Swords, Fortune, the ten of Disks, the Queen of Swords and the five of Cups.

"The killer is clever, a master of disguise, hiding from recognition."

Impatient, Rebecca said, "Tell me something I don't already know."

After taking a moment to study the cards, Odette locked gazes with her. "The murderer," she finally said, "is the one with the most to gain."

Rebecca sighed. "Appropriately cryptic." What else had she expected?

"Tarot is not an exact science," Odette said.

Tarot wasn't science of any kind, but Rebecca wasn't going to say so. Odette was put off by her presence as it was. Better to humor her.

"Most to gain," she mused aloud. "That could mean anything."

"The ten of Disks indicates wealth."

"Money is always a strong motivation for murder. But who would make money from the deaths of the people in your voodoo group?"

"You no longer need to worry your head about that."

"It's my job to worry about it. And to find the real killer."

"I'll be making sure the murders stop," Odette said, "with the help of the *loa.*"

Rebecca stared at the priestess. She was serious. She believed she could do it. Gooseflesh rose along Rebecca's arms. Maybe Odette could prevent future murders—if voodoo really worked.

''I heard you were planning a ceremony,'' Rebecca prompted.

''Tomorrow night,'' Odette admitted. ''St. John's Eve holds powerful magic. Tomorrow night, all will be resolved.''

A choking sound from the voodoo room made Rebecca turn in time to see Marie scurry out through the back exit. Apparently the assistant was upset. She must be a believer.

Rebecca felt the skin along her spine crawl as she wondered how much of a believer she herself was.

ZACH WAS FILLING OUT paperwork on an arrest when Becca waltzed into the station. Spotting him, she gave a small wave as if their relationship hadn't done a one-eighty the night before, and quickly made for her own desk. He gave her a few minutes, but she didn't even look his way.

What had he expected after she'd ducked out on him that morning without waking him?

Still steaming that she could act as though nothing had happened between them, he figured two could play that game and made his way over to her desk.

''Any breaking news I should know about?'' he asked in a low impersonal voice.

''I paid Odette a visit this morning. The Tarot cards told her that the murderer is the one with the most to gain.''

She sounded skeptical, but Zachary had great respect for the paranormal arts. Not that most of the boasting by those that practiced them wasn't just that. Boasting. Lies. Loads of individuals in New Orleans made their living giving tourists a thrill they could talk about when they got home. But Odette LaFantary was a different story. She had a reputation for being the genuine article.

"Most to gain. That would describe Miss Lulu inheriting the DeLyon fortune." Having called Liam the night before once Becca had fallen asleep, Zachary wondered if his brother was making any headway with her stepchildren. "But I don't think we should count out Helen Gaylord or Lisa Cantro just yet."

"I'm not counting out anyone," she said.

"No?" She'd certainly counted *him* out fast enough. "What do you say we start with Lisa? After work?"

She hesitated. Because she didn't want to work with him? Zachary wondered. Because she regretted last night? Refusing to let her see him bothered, he sat there wearing a neutral expression that he'd developed early on in life. Emotional protection. Finally she nodded and he said he'd pick her up at her place at the agreed-on time.

He returned to his paperwork and tried to put Becca out of mind for the rest of the day.

Fat chance.

By the time they arrived at Lisa Cantro's, the sun had set and he was wound up tight. And from the tension emanating his way, he figured Becca felt the same. With at least a foot of space between them, they made their way through an opening into an inner courtyard and found the right apartment.

Zachary's knock was followed by a crash from inside, making him think another voodoo regular was in trouble. After all, Lisa had already received a gris-gris. He pulled his gun. "Open up! Police."

Seconds later, the door swung open to reveal a distraught Lisa, who looked as if she'd been pulling out her hair. And destroying her apartment, considering the mess behind her. Couch cushions were strewn all over, magazines were ripped apart, and a vase lay smashed on the floor.

''I don't need any more problems,'' Lisa muttered, turning her back on them.

''What is it?'' Becca asked, entering the apartment. ''What happened in here?''

Seeming too distracted to make sense of the questions, Lisa pulled out an end-table drawer and dumped its contents on the tabletop. ''I've got to find it!'' She sorted through the mess, making sounds of exasperation.

''Is this something to do with the murders?'' Zachary asked.

''Murders?'' She looked up. ''No! The spell Odette cast for my good fortune worked. I bought a lottery ticket with winning numbers and now I've misplaced the damn thing!'' She pulled out another drawer and began sorting through it. ''That ticket is worth nearly four thousand dollars, and believe me, I could use that money.''

Registering the fact that Odette's spell had worked, Zachary pulled Becca back. ''I don't think we're going to get what we need here tonight,'' he said to her.

''Maybe we should go on to Helen's.''

At least they agreed on something.

Zachary wished Lisa good luck and Becca said they'd catch up with her another time. Lisa didn't seem to hear or notice when they made their way out.

''Let's hope Helen Gaylord is more helpful,'' he said.

Hating to bother the elderly woman, what with her sister Sadie dead and all, he steeled himself on the short drive to her home. But he didn't have to worry about bothering her. Helen appeared happy to see them, and chatty, too, as if pleased to have company.

"May I offer you refreshments?" she asked after they took seats in her fussy parlor. "Lemonade, perhaps?"

"Nothing," Zach said. "We just want to talk to you about the murders, see if there's something you remember that can help us catch the killer."

"I knew it wasn't that nice Jordan O'Reilly. But now I don't think we're going to have anything to worry about after tomorrow night."

"The voodoo ceremony?" Becca asked.

Helen nodded. "Odette's spells are so powerful, getting people out of wheelchairs, helping them win lotteries, connecting with the past..."

"We can't leave this to chance," Becca said. "Before she died, Sadie called Camille DuPree and said she knew something about DeLyon's murder, but then your sister was killed before Camille caught up to her. Did Sadie by any chance confide in you whatever she wanted Camille to know?"

Helen raised her penciled brows and said huffily, "Sadie confided more to her diary than she did to her own sister."

"Diary?" Becca echoed. "You didn't mention any diary before."

"Yes, I did. I told Detective Yancy, but he didn't seem interested."

Yancy again.

"If *you* think it's important, Helen, then we're interested," Zachary said. "Maybe we could have a peek?"

"Of course."

A few minutes later, nearly head-to-head with Becca, Zachary had difficulty concentrating on the contents of the diary. He was too aware of her, too filled with memories of the night before.

How would this night end? he wondered.

Then she mumbled, "This is odd. Look, right after Janet Phillippe died, Sadie writes, 'Too bad Janet's daughter can't believe how much her mama got out of the voodoo group. She feels cheated.'"

Zachary felt his hackles rise at that one. He knew Janet Phillippe had been one of the original members of the voodoo group but had died of natural causes the month before. And then one by one, the others began to die. He didn't believe in coincidence.

"Janet's daughter," he said. "I've never heard her mentioned before."

"Me, neither," Becca said. "What about you, Helen?"

The old lady shook her head, making her silver-blue curls quiver. "Janet was estranged from the girl. Said she didn't believe in voodoo, thought it was all nonsense. I don't think Sadie actually ever met her. She must've been repeating something Janet told her."

"So the daughter never came to one of Odette's voodoo ceremonies?"

"Not that I know of."

Another dead end?

THE VISIT with Helen ended, Rebecca found herself back in the car, with Zach in charge behind the wheel once more.

"You will take me to *my* home this time, right?" she asked.

"If that's what you want." When she didn't respond, he said, "I think we should add Janet's daughter to the list of suspects. We'll need her name for starters."

"Odette may know who she is." Rebecca pulled out her cell phone and placed the call, only to encounter Odette's voice mail. She left a message, then said, "That's it for tonight, I guess."

"If that's what you want," he said again.

Butterflies attacked her stomach. How to respond to his prompting? Zach didn't fool her. He'd been playing it cool all day. At first she'd been irritated that he could act so normal, as if nothing had happened between them. Then she realized he'd simply been taking his cue from her.

That was good, she told herself. No, great. It was a relief. No pressure. Gave her time to think.

"Becca, we need to talk."

"If only we had something concrete," she said, knowing he didn't mean the case, but desperate to keep him at a distance. "Maybe when Odette gets back to me with that name and Liam gets back to you about the DeLyon clan…"

She swore she could hear Zach grinding his teeth, but he didn't take another stab at anything personal, thank goodness. Instead, he remained silent for the rest of the drive.

When they arrived at her place, Rebecca jumped out of the car, saying, "Let me know if you hear anything and I'll do the same."

Zach grunted and got out, too. Uh-oh. Dismayed, Rebecca stiffened and headed up the walk to the small house she shared with her mom, who was currently out of town visiting her sister. Surely Zach wouldn't insist on coming in.

"Hey, what's that?" he asked.

She followed his gaze to a fancy beaded box perched

on the stoop. The jewel tones gleamed invitingly under the soft porch light.

"Odette sells those boxes at her shop. She acted kind of cool earlier. Maybe she left it as an apology."

As she reached for it, Rebecca was startled when Zach shouted, "No!" and pulled it out of her hands.

"Hey, what did you do that for?"

Before he could answer, the lid popped open. Zach grunted and dropped the box, and she saw a flash of movement.

A slithering snake.

Chapter Seven

Another snake!

Heart pounding, Rebecca barely got a glimpse of the viper as it slithered off. "Odette uses snakes in her act. This one's a copperhead." She turned to Zach and realized he was holding on to his hand. "Oh, no—it bit you!"

"I'm aware of that."

Even though copperhead bites weren't fatal if treated in time, she felt a rising panic. If something happened to Zach… She couldn't bear the thought.

"Just what I need," he complained, as if he wasn't worried. "A trip to the emergency room tonight."

Maybe he was just trying not to worry her.

"You can't go alone."

"Why not?"

"Don't be a hero. Not now. And stand still. Don't move this arm," she said, bending his elbow and flattening it across his chest.

"You're a snake-bite expert?"

"I learned a few things about emergencies in Girl Scouts," she muttered, starting to remove his belt.

"Um, isn't this a little public, *chère?*"

"Don't get your hopes up." Pulling his belt free, she

took off hers and secured them together. Then she used them to bind his arm to his torso so he couldn't move it and spread the venom. "There," she said, taking a big breath. "Give me your car keys."

Zach didn't fight her in any way, but slipped into the passenger seat meekly. Rebecca wondered if Zach's taking orders from her without comment was reason to worry. Her hand was trembling when she started the engine, and her chest felt uncomfortably tight. But surely he would be okay.

She assured herself of that over and over while making small talk with Zach as she drove straight for the nearest hospital. Five minutes later they were in the emergency room and he was in competent hands, so she could breathe easier.

While he was being treated, she called in the incident and told the desk sergeant to have the box, which was still on the walkway, picked up as evidence. Then she checked her voice mail to see if Odette had left a message, but was disappointed. She tried Odette again and left an even more urgent message.

What if the box had been from Odette's shop? What if the snake had belonged to her? Yancy had suspected the woman until he'd turned on Jordan, but Rebecca had never believed that her old friend was capable of murder.

Had she been wrong?

When the responding officer arrived at the hospital, he said he'd searched the grounds in front of her house, but hadn't found the box. Well, Rebecca thought, either some passerby had picked it up or the killer had been watching them and had retrieved the evidence.

Suddenly the incident hit home, big time. Zach hadn't been the intended victim. *She* had. Her mouth went dry and her pulse pounded. The Voodoo Killer was after *her* now. Why? Because she was on the case? But why not Yancy? The message was clear—the killer was trying to stop her because she wasn't going along with Yancy's program. Because she was getting too close.

To whom? Odette?

"Excuse me, Detective Romero?"

"Yes." She popped out of her chair and faced one of the nurses. "Is Zach...Officer Doucet all right?"

"He's doing fine. The doctor wants to keep him overnight for observation."

Taking a big breath, Rebecca felt the pressure in her chest ease up. "Can I see him?"

"Certainly."

Zach was the only patient in a semiprivate room. She stood by the doorway and let the responding officer take his statement first. Zach kept glancing her way, and Rebecca had a sick feeling, seeing him so vulnerable and lying in that bed, one arm bandaged, the other connected to an IV. She waited until the nurse took his vitals before entering.

"You look tired, *chère*," Zach said, sounding more personal than he had all night. "You should go home and get some sleep."

"Not yet."

Filled with guilt that Zach had been bitten by a snake meant for her, Rebecca knew she couldn't leave him. She didn't want to face the other emotions brewing in her. There'd been a crushing weight on her chest when she'd seen the viper, a weight that went beyond fear for a fellow human being.

Time to admit she'd never gotten over her feelings for Zach...

"You're the one who looks tired," she said, taking

a chair next to his bed. "I'll just sit here for a minute, while you close your eyes and dream."

Smiling, he closed his eyes as ordered and murmured, "Every time I dream, I dream of you."

A thrill shot through her. "Flatterer."

Could he be telling the truth? Could she mean as much to him as he did to her?

Zach's breathing grew deeper. Rebecca relaxed and allowed herself to watch his face in repose. She loved every familiar plane and angle, and it took all her willpower not to reach out and touch him lest she wake him.

She loved him.

Her heart lurched even as she faced the inevitable truth, one she'd been avoiding since that morning: she was in love with Zachary Doucet, had been since they'd worked together, and she didn't know what to do about it.

Resting her head against the chair, she continued staring at him until exhaustion caught up to her, and her own eyes fluttered closed....

She awoke once in the middle of the night to find Zach's fingers entwined with hers. He'd rolled over and reached out for her in his sleep. Sighing, she gave his hand a squeeze and closed her eyes again.

The next time she awoke it was to see Zach lying on his side and staring at her, his gaze open and vulnerable. For a heart-stopping second, she recognized something there, something that made her want to tell him how she felt—and then a knock at the door tore their gazes apart.

Rebecca glanced over to the doorway. Liam stood there, and for just a second, before he put a neutral expression in place, she saw his true feelings. Seeing

Zach in the hospital bed upset him more than he cared to admit.

Maybe he didn't hate his brother, after all.

SURPRISED TO SEE Liam, Zachary said, "Come on in. Take a seat."

Liam moved closer but remained on the far side of the bed from Becca. "Word at the station is you tried to get friendly with a snake last night. But, uh, the nurse told me you're going to live, anyway."

"So they say."

He and Liam held each other's gazes for a moment, and Zachary thought he saw something in his half brother's that hadn't been there previously.

Then Liam looked away from him toward Becca. "Hey, thanks for going beyond the call of duty."

Wondering if he meant helping to clear Jordan's name or staying with *him* all night, Zachary said, "My heroine," in that slightly mocking tone meant to put Becca off her stride, which was just the way he liked her.

Liam cleared his throat. "I spoke to DeLyon's older son and daughter."

That got Zachary's full attention. "And?"

"And they're understandably angry that Miss Lulu cheated them of their inheritance and are planning on going to court."

"Cheated," Zachary echoed. "That's what Sadie said about Janet Phillippe's daughter—that she felt cheated by the voodoo group."

"Sadie? When?"

"In her diary," Becca said. "We paid Helen a visit last night and she gave us a look-see. Apparently Helen made Yancy the same offer."

"Undoubtedly he turned it down because he didn't want any information that would take the heat off Jordan," Liam guessed.

"Who *is* Janet's daughter, anyway?" Zachary asked.

Liam shrugged. "Got me. Janet wasn't murdered, though. René Badeaux swears she died of old age—heart failure. The only reason René did the autopsy was because the daughter was convinced the old lady was murdered. Of course she also said that voodoo was involved. But in the end, the autopsy didn't turn up anything suspicious."

"Voodoo, huh?" Zachary mused aloud. "Still, the daughter suspected foul play. Maybe I should talk with her when they let me out of here. René might have her name and address."

"Hey, take it easy. A snakebite's nothing to fool with." Liam frowned. "I think I'll rattle Odette's cage about the copperhead. And maybe see if Janet paid her big bucks for some gris-gris or hex or something."

"If you can find her," Becca said. "I've tried calling her a couple of times. She seems to be incommunicado."

"Maybe you ought to go with Liam," Zachary suggested.

"Odette is my friend, but I'm not leaving you alone."

That she sounded torn but had chosen *him* made Zach's chest tighten. "Promise?" he asked softly.

Their gazes locked, his mouth went dry, and then, as if coming out of a trance, she blinked and looked away.

"Not until the twenty-four hours runs out and I know for sure you're in the clear." She shrugged as if it was nothing, saying, "Someone has to keep an eye on you."

The good feeling dissipated. So she thought someone had to keep an eye on him, did she? Obviously she still didn't trust him.

REBECCA DROVE Zach to work, all the while wishing something so important didn't rest on their pursuing this information immediately. But tomorrow could be too late. Who knew what would happen at Odette's ceremony that evening? They couldn't let anyone else die.

The moment they walked into the station, Gary Yancy pounced on her. ''Where the hell have you been, Romero? Do you know what time it is?''

''I called in and spoke to the lieutenant. He didn't tell you?''

''He told me, all right.'' Yancy straightened the cuffs of his lime-green sports jacket. ''I've heard other things, too, like you're still investigating the Voodoo Killer when we already have him behind bars.''

''We don't,'' Zach said.

''What business is it of yours, Doucet? Oh, yeah, that blood business. Keep your nose outta my case.''

Zach tensed beside her, but Rebecca put an arm out to keep him back. ''Do you have any new information for me?'' she asked Yancy.

His jaw worked. ''No.'' And then he stalked off.

Amazed that he'd given up the fight so easily, Rebecca stared after him. ''Well, that went better than I thought it would.''

''The man's a discredit to the department.''

''If only we could make others see that.''

''He's a waste of time,'' Zach said. ''Let's sign in and then go see René.''

The morgue wasn't Rebecca's favorite place, and so she was glad when they caught the assistant coroner in his office. The room was decorated with anatomy posters and, in one corner, a real human skeleton.

"Zachary Doucet and Rebecca Romero, together again." René couldn't hide his surprise. "What brings you to see me?"

"The Voodoo Killer," Zach said.

"Shoulda known." René looked at Rebecca. "Yancy tell you about Danielle Ambrose?"

"Who?"

"Janet Phillippe's daughter, the one who made all the fuss about my doing an autopsy on the old lady."

"What about the daughter?" she asked. "You've heard from her again?"

"No. But after that conversation with Liam and Simone Jones, I kept wondering why the woman was so certain her mother was murdered. Then I learned that Miss Ambrose was cut out of her mother's will."

Zach asked, "What does that have to do with the Voodoo Killer?"

"If Danielle Ambrose isn't inheriting, who is?"

"Oh, my God. The diary. Janet's daughter felt cheated by the voodoo group." Rebecca's mind was spinning with the possibilities. "One of them must have been named in the will. And you told Yancy this?"

"He said he'd take it under consideration."

"He lied to me!" Rebecca exclaimed. "I asked if there were any new developments and he said no. So how do we find out who inherited?"

"The daughter knows."

René gave them the address and they were off.

Danielle Ambrose lived on the second floor of a modern apartment building in the adjoining suburb of Metarie. Ringing her doorbell got no response.

"Maybe we should have called first," Rebecca said, then checked her watch. "She's probably at work."

"You lookin' for Danielle?" asked a dusky-skinned woman coming out of the next apartment. She eyed Zach's uniform, then appeared sorry she'd spoken up.

He gave her one of those slow syrupy smiles that made Rebecca's knees go weak and said, "Don't worry, she's not in trouble." But when he went on, "We need to tell her the good news about her late mother's estate," Rebecca stiffened. "There's a big inheritance waiting for her. All she has to do is show up to claim it. So can you tell us where to find her, *chère*?"

He was doing it again, not only charming the woman, but lying to get information out of her. Rebecca swallowed hard so that she didn't call him on it.

And indeed the neighbor softened enough to tell him, "Danielle said she was goin' on another business trip, but she ain't been back in weeks."

"She goes on a lot of business trips?"

"Ever since she moved in a couple months ago, she's hardly ever here. But this time, it's like she…well, like she up and disappeared."

Unfortunately that was the extent of the woman's knowledge. She had no idea where Danielle worked.

Back in the car with Rebecca behind the wheel again, Zach said, "We need a photograph of this Danielle Ambrose. Maybe Miss Lulu or Lisa Cantro or Helen would recognize her."

Though Rebecca agreed, she asked, "So what are you going to do next? Put out an all-points on the woman so that you can get the information you need?"

She could feel Zach's gaze on her before he asked, "Do you have a problem with me?"

"Why can't you ever play it straight?"

"Whoa. Are you telling me you never stretched the truth to get information on a case?" When she sat, jaw clenched, unable to deny it, he said, "Uh-huh," and lapsed into silence.

Gripping the wheel tightly, Rebecca assured herself that she wasn't being unfair. She knew cops often lied to get suspects to talk. She'd stretched the truth herself a few times, but she had boundaries she didn't cross.

What now? Who would know about the will and Danielle Ambrose other than Odette? Odette was still suspect—and probably still unavailable, no doubt preparing for that night's ceremony.

"We need to talk to someone about the will," Zach said, his mind obviously in synch with hers. "Someone who likes to talk."

"Helen," they said as one.

"So, are you going to let me handle this my way, or do we have to straight-arrow it?"

Rebecca took a deep breath before saying, "Your way."

Maybe she had been too sensitive about how he'd handled the Ambrose woman's neighbor. And he did have a way with Helen. Probably with most women. Every lead helped, and hopefully Helen would be more forthcoming than she'd been the night before.

But when they got to her place, the elderly woman was in a flurry about what outfit to wear for that evening's voodoo ceremony.

Standing in the foyer, she held up a plain red dress in one hand, and a sparkly black dress in the other. "Which one should I wear?" she asked Zach.

"Close your eyes and pick, *chère*. You'll be equally lovely in both."

To Rebecca's chagrin, Helen actually giggled girlishly.

"But before you start getting ready," she said, "maybe you could answer a few more questions?"

Helen sighed. "It isn't really necessary, because tonight Odette's going to create a spell strong enough to stop the murders."

"Until she does, we need to keep investigating," Rebecca said to pacify her. "Where is she going to hold this ceremony?"

"I'm not supposed to say."

"At Camille DuPree's restaurant?"

"No!"

"No one is going to get in trouble," Zach said soothingly. "This is the Big Easy, *chère*. Anyone who doesn't believe in voodoo…" He shook his head.

"You believe?"

"I learned at my mama's knee. I can't think of anything I would rather do tonight."

"Well…the ceremony will be out on the bayou."

"Not on St. John's Bayou where Marie Laveau held her ceremonies?" Rebecca asked caustically. "That isn't possible anymore."

"No, not there. A wild stretch Odette inherited outside of town—" Helen stopped and pursed her lips as if she'd said too much already.

Apparently the elderly woman wasn't going to clarify the location of the land, so Rebecca switched direction. "Who was named beneficiary in Janet Phillippe's will?"

Going pale, Helen backed up a step. "I…I didn't kill anyone."

"*You* inherited the money?"

Helen looked from one to the other. "We all did.

Odette and the rest of us. Janet remembered *all* her friends. Those of us who are still alive to collect when the estate finally gets settled, that is.''

''What about the money left to Spiro DeLyon and Tony Fortune and your sister?'' Zach asked. ''Do the rest of you get that, too?''

Shrugging, Helen avoided their eyes. ''I didn't kill anyone.''

Wondering what else the woman might be hiding, Rebecca asked, ''Why didn't you tell us about the will last night?''

''Y-you didn't ask.''

Chapter Eight

"So we have a handful of people who are considerably wealthier with each death," Zachary said as they headed for the car. He was trying to keep his mind on business rather than on Becca's distrust of him. "That takes suspicion away from the daughter and back to the voodoo group. So which one is greedy enough to want it all?"

"Or what if they all die?" Becca mused. "What if the daughter isn't really on vacation but disappeared the way the neighbor indicated because she's busy wreaking revenge for getting left out of her mother's will?"

"So if they all die, what happens to the money?" Zach continued. "Maybe the estate reverts to the daughter automatically."

"If not, she can always go to court and sue for the money. We need to find her."

"You're right. We can't count her out. We need that photograph."

On the way back to the station, they picked up some fast food at a drive-through. Munching on fried oysters with hot sauce, Zachary called in a request for Danielle Ambrose's Department of Motor Vehicles records, which included a photograph, but before he had a chance to put away the cell phone, a call came in from Liam.

"Someone tried to kill Lisa Cantro. She's okay, though, and about to leave the emergency room."

"What happened?"

"She was going out to run a few errands before heading to the voodoo ceremony and was attacked from behind. Apparently the neighbor's barking dogs saved her. She said someone's been shadowing her since she got the gris-gris. Whoever it was spooked her good in the cemetery the other night—the night Tony Fortune died. She thinks *she* was the intended target."

"Did she see her attacker's face?"

"No. She swears it's a woman, though. Said she smelled an exotic scent, bergamot mixed with ginger. Said she could ID it because she smells it every time she goes into Odette's shop."

Zachary related Liam's news to Becca, who agreed they didn't have time to go back to the station. They needed to get to that voodoo ceremony.

"But first we have to find the site. Maybe Helen can be of more help than she offered," he suggested. "She can lead us there without knowing it."

Agreeing, Becca drove back to the elderly woman's house and parked half a block away, where they could see her leave. Zachary popped the last oyster in his mouth while she took a bite of her burger and a long sip of soda.

"Land Odette inherited…" she mused aloud, setting the drink in a holder.

"Part of Janet Phillippe's estate?"

"I was wondering the same thing. I don't like to think Odette could be guilty of murder. I've known her forever and I'd swear that, voodoo priestess or not, she doesn't have an evil bone in her body.''

"Voodoo doesn't automatically mean black magic.''

"I know that. But now Lisa said she recognized the scent from Taboo. Who else…?''

"Doesn't Odette have someone working for her?''

"Yes, but Marie Germain is new. The first time I met her was a couple of weeks ago when I stopped by the shop to pick up some bath salts. What would be her motive?''

"Are we certain her name really *is* Marie Germain?''

"You're suggesting she might be…''

"Danielle Ambrose? Why not?''

They sank into silence as they finished eating. Zachary tried to concentrate on whether Odette's assistant could be the missing daughter, a difficult task with Becca next to him. He couldn't forget the night they'd spent together with nothing—certainly not the past—between them.

So when she said that she hated waiting, he replied, "You hate a lot of things.''

"Meaning?''

"Me.''

"I don't hate you, Zach. I…''

Though it sounded as if Becca had more to say, she didn't. But he wasn't going to let her drop it.

"My way of doing things, then,'' he said.

"All right. I don't always agree with the way you do things.''

"Tell me what I did on this case that was out of line.''

She met his gaze. "You con people.''

"Every cop uses his wits to get information, Becca,''

he said, moving closer to her. "You couldn't deny it yourself."

He heard her breathing change. Maybe his nearness was affecting her. Good.

Still, she said, "You skirt the edge—"

"Not anymore, I don't. When that twig hit the fan and I lost you, *chère,* I reevaluated my way of doing things. You just haven't been around to notice."

When she opened her mouth as if to protest, he took the advantage and brushed his lips over hers. She sat there stiffly but didn't move away. Encouraged, he tried again. Sighing this time, as if she couldn't help herself, she leaned in to him. He angled his mouth over hers and kissed her deeply, trying to convey everything he felt for her.

The kiss was slow and wet and so erotic that it jump-started his erection.

But before he could do anything about it, she pushed him away. They stared at each other for a moment before Zachary slid back to his side of the car. She'd given over for a moment, but it was as if she'd put some kind of shield back in place.

"What's the real problem, Becca? Why is it you don't trust me?"

She looked away from him, then tensed. "Helen's leaving the house." She started the car.

And ended the conversation she so obviously didn't want to have.

VOODOO PRACTITIONERS from all over New Orleans gathered to celebrate the summer solstice. Even before Marie Laveau's reign, St. John's Eve was always their most important date to revel and cast spells. Although she wasn't a believer, Rebecca couldn't help being af-

fected by the charged atmosphere as dusk fell over the
bayou and the waning moon presided over the spectacle.
It gave her something to think about other than Zach's
challenge about why she didn't trust him with herself.

Standing under a moss-draped cypress tree at the
edge of a clearing, she and Zach watched the celebrants
already in action.

There were dozens of them and more were arriving.
Some dressed in street clothes added wood to the bonfire at the edge of the bayou. Others in flowing garments
and masks drummed or clapped a rhythm for the dancers. Several men in loincloths and more women in white
cotton shifts, their heads wrapped with white cloth,
dipped and twirled around the flames while drinking
from a flask they passed around.

Overseeing the voodoo gala from a thronelike chair
set on a box, Odette was draped in what looked like
white handkerchiefs. And a boa constrictor. She stroked
the snake as if it was a beloved pet.

"I've never been to one of these ceremonies before,"
Rebecca admitted with a little shiver.

Zach didn't say anything.

On edge after what had happened between them in
the car, knowing he would pick up that conversation the
first chance he got, she scanned the crowd for familiar
faces. She found the regulars—Helen, of course, and
Lisa and Miss Lulu all in street clothes. But Odette's
assistant, Marie, was nowhere to be seen. Perhaps she
was one of the masked participants or one of the dancers, and was simply unrecognizable.

Continuing to pass the flask, the dancers snaked from
the bonfire to surround Odette. The drink seemed to be
affecting them, making their movements and gestures
wilder.

"I wonder what they're drinking," Rebecca murmured as the rest of the celebrants migrated in that direction.

"Traditionally, it would be *tafia,* a crude alcoholic drink distilled from molasses," Zach said, leaning so close that she shivered for another reason. "But considering the times, it might simply be rum."

The music thumped louder and faster and the dancers appeared to be working themselves into a frenzy. Rebecca felt her nerves grow even more taut. Why was it she *didn't* trust Zach with herself? He deserved an answer and she knew he would press her until she gave him one. Perhaps because his style of investigation was more slippery than hers, she feared he would treat *her* that way.

When he suggested, "Maybe we should split up, look for anything suspicious," she felt the tension in her middle ease a bit.

She nodded. "I'll look for Marie Germain."

Zach moved toward the people around the bonfire while she edged toward the dancers.

Moonlight cast a sheen on their skin, damp with humidity and sweat. Suddenly a woman seemed overcome by some spirit. Her body jerked and trembled and she whirled faster and faster in a circle. Another dancer joined her and then another. Still others, men and women both, pulled off their garments and ran naked into the bayou, where despite the presence of alligators, they shook and shrieked and splashed themselves with cooling waters.

A piercing scream made Rebecca turn. Right behind her, a woman lay on the ground convulsing, her eyes rolling back in her head, apparently possessed by the *loa.*

The sight made Rebecca's skin crawl. Maybe there was more to this voodoo than she'd ever conceded.

Rebecca backed up, putting distance between herself and what she didn't understand—straight into waiting arms. A swath of material folded around her, and too quickly for her to struggle, a cloth with a sweet sickly smell covered her mouth and nose. Gasping, she couldn't take a breath.

And then her reality shifted so that the sound and energy surrounding her faded into a distant whisper.

SCOURING THE GROUNDS for what? Zachary asked himself. Nothing seemed overtly suspicious here.

He soon became frustrated with his fruitless search. They needed that damn photograph. More and more it made sense that Janet Phillippe's daughter was the one they should be looking for.

Since he couldn't do that, he tried to find Becca, but she seemed to have disappeared.

He'd circled the whole area twice when Odette rose from her throne and lifted the boa with both hands. The celebrants swirled around him and past him and watched their priestess eagerly as if for a cue. And, like zombies summoned by their mistress, those splashing in the bayou left the water.

"We are gathered here tonight to banish evil from our midst," the priestess intoned in a compelling voice. "Banish evil!"

"Banish evil!" her congregants repeated.

"Officer Doucet?"

He turned to see Lisa Cantro. She cut through the crowd, and just as she got to him, someone bumped into her, making them collide. They grappled with each other for a moment, trying to restore their balance amidst the teeming crowd, then he helped her right herself.

"Should you be here?" he asked. "I understand you were attacked earlier."

Odette's voice was growing more powerful. "There is a murderer in our midst—one who would see true believers dead. We must protect ourselves."

"Protect...protect...protect..."

Lisa turned her back on the others and gripped Zachary's arm. "This is a ceremony of vengeance. After what happened to me, I had to be here. But that doesn't matter now. I saw you with Detective Romero..."

"What about her?"

Odette's voice boomed in the night. "We need to stop the killings, to see that justice is done!"

Distracted, Lisa glanced back at the other celebrants as they echoed, "Justice...justice..." but then pointed over his shoulder and said, "I saw someone drag off Detective Romero over there."

His gut seized in a knot of dread, Zachary glanced at a part of the bayou where the alligators had been disturbed by all the noise. As he watched, one slid from the far bank into the water.

"Who took her?" he asked Lisa.

"The person was wearing a cape and a mask."

Zach took off running, Odette's voice carrying through the night after him.

"I summon the *loa* to guide me, to give me the power, to let me use the collected force of this gathering to bring an end to evil this night."

Then the chanting began, dozens of male and female voices raising together in some strange French text he didn't even try to decipher.

He spotted a dark shape at the bank of the bayou nearly hidden by tall duckbill grass. Becca?

As he raced toward her, he saw that she lay face-down, her legs half in the water, her hands tied behind her back. An alligator was gliding through the water toward her. They were fast creatures, but a bullet was faster. He reached behind him for his gun, but the holster was empty.

"What the hell!"

The alligator was almost upon Becca.

Instincts kicking in, Zachary grabbed up a broken tree branch and lunged forward, whacking the alligator on the nose. A young one and easily discouraged, it turned away long enough for him to pull the woman he loved well away from the water's edge.

"Becca! Becca, wake up!" he yelled over the cacophony of chanting.

He untied her hands and shook her gently. Her eyes fluttered open and she spit water as she croaked, "Zach!"

She was going to be all right. "Let me help you sit up."

Not as easy as it sounded. She seemed to be fighting her way to consciousness. Perhaps she'd been drugged. But somehow he got her upright and in his embrace. He held her tightly, never wanting to let her go. Her arms slid around his neck and she shuddered against his chest.

"You found me," Becca murmured. "I thought I was a goner."

"I wouldn't let you leave me," he said fiercely, just as he heard a noise behind him.

"My, my, isn't this sweet?"

With his arms still wrapped around the woman he loved, Zachary turned to face the murderess who he now realized had bumped into him purposely moments ago.

Lisa Cantro was holding his gun on them.

Chapter Nine

Suddenly the chanting stopped and the complete silence made Rebecca's skin crawl. Her head was woozy with whatever she'd inhaled that had knocked her out, but she forced herself to concentrate.

Lisa seemed nervous even as she said, "You two made a big mistake. You should never have involved yourself in something that wasn't your business."

Zach got to his feet and stood protectively in front of Rebecca. "Jordan O'Reilly is my brother."

Ignoring that, Lisa said, "Odette and her groupies cheated me of my rightful inheritance, and they need to be punished."

Rebecca choked out, "You're Danielle Ambrose."

"So you figured it out."

"It's my job."

Odette's voice rose from the clearing once more. "Hear me now, murderer! The gods and the saints are with us…"

Fighting the last of the knockout drug, Rebecca took several deep cleansing breaths. The woman was crazy enough to shoot them both. Gathering her strength, Rebecca pushed up from the squishy earth and staggered to her feet.

"Stay right there," Danielle shouted.

"Or you'll what?" Zach asked, moving away from Rebecca. "Shoot me? Aren't you planning on doing that, anyway?"

A click echoed across the bayou—Lisa/Danielle taking the safety off. Apparently she knew how to use a revolver.

And Rebecca knew what he was doing. He was drawing fire away from her. He was going to make sure that if one of them had to take a bullet, it wouldn't be her.

Why is it you don't trust me? he'd asked her.

The fog in her brain slid away and with it her doubts. More magic? She trusted Zach to be brave and foolish and maybe get himself killed to save her.

She couldn't let him do that.

Odette's voice continued to echo around them— "Your evil has angered all, angered the deities, and we call an end to your reign…"—a distracted Danielle was breathing heavily, and suddenly Rebecca knew she had to use Zach's methods to save them both.

"You might as well give up, Danielle," Rebecca said. "You can't get away with this. You're being recorded. We knew the murderer would show up, so we set up videocams ahead of time."

"Video…uh-uh, it's too dark!"

"They're infrared," Rebecca lied.

As the chanting started up again, Danielle looked around wildly as if trying to see the cameras. Rebecca lunged for her, but Danielle ducked and grabbed her arm. A muzzy-headed Rebecca fought to get free, but she was no match for the crazed murderer. Danielle jammed the gun barrel in her side hard, and there was nothing Rebecca could do but freeze.

"Don't do this, *chère,*" Zach said in his most seductive voice. "Killing a citizen is one thing. Killing a cop is another. You'll have the whole department down on you. There'll be no saving you then."

"You don't think I'm going to let you spoil everything now, do you?"

Rebecca said, "The cameras—"

Danielle cut her off, yelling, "Liar!"

Zach continued to move so that Danielle had to move also, lest he get behind her. Rebecca watched for an opportunity, but the pressure in her side didn't let up.

"The New Orleans police will never figure it out," Danielle bragged.

"Ah, but, *chère,* we figured it out."

"But you'll be gone and Detective Yancy will be running the case his way. He'll pin it on O'Reilly like he's been doing all along. And I'll be a rich woman. I can simply take the money and disappear and no one will ever notice. Stop moving!"

Zach ignored her and continued on. They'd come full circle, Rebecca realized.

Odette's chanting reached them again. "I call on the deities to act on our behalf…"

"You have another problem, *chère.* The voodoo gods. If Odette is angry with you, then *they're* angry with you."

"A-angry? No."

But she sounded worried, Rebecca realized. "If Odette brings a curse down on you," she said, "well, heaven help you."

Zach stared at Danielle. "But maybe it's not too late—"

"Shut up, both of you!"

Zach lunged to the side and Danielle turned with him. Feeling the gun barrel pull away slightly, Rebecca planted herself and jabbed back as hard as she could. Aware of Zach rushing forward as her elbow made contact with Danielle's soft middle, she was horrified when the gun fired.

He kept coming.

"Take her soul before someone else dies," Odette's voice called.

"No, no one's going to get my soul!" Danielle screamed as Zach grabbed her, and Rebecca fell on the spongy ground.

Catching her breath, she watched with horror as the murderer and the man she loved danced around with the gun between them. If the gun went off again...

Odette commanded the gods, "Stop this evil *now!*"

The word *now* seemed to echo through the night.

Danielle made a strangled sound. Her eyes widened and her expression turned into one of horror. Her body jerked and she tried to speak, but her voice was garbled. Then the horror faded and her whole body went still...just as if her soul had fled her body, leaving her a zombie.

Finding her cross at her throat, Rebecca held on to it and said a quick prayer for the woman.

Was Odette really powerful enough to turn someone into the walking dead? Or was Danielle's own belief in voodoo enough to do it?

AFTER HANDCUFFING Danielle to a log, Zachary pulled Becca into his arms. "I don't know what I would have done if she'd hurt you." He kissed her forehead and her nose. "I really thought she was going to shoot you." He kissed one cheek, then the other. "Thank God you're all right."

"Because of you."

"And because you lied, *chère*." He couldn't help giving her a hard time. "I thought you had boundaries."

"I knew if I didn't do something, you would get yourself killed to protect me. I was desperate."

"I was desperate when she jammed that gun in your—"

"Shh, listen," Becca suddenly said. "The chanting stopped."

Around them, the night had gone still.

They both glanced to where Janet Phillippe's daughter sat passively, her vacant eyes staring.

Though he was reluctant to let Becca out of his arms, Zachary said, "We need to call this in." He reached for his radio, but she stopped him.

"Wait. First I need to tell you…I do trust you, Zach. I was simply afraid you might play fast and loose with my heart."

"I would never do that, *chère,* not with you."

"I realize now I was wrong. And I need to admit something else. I…I've had feelings for you forever. I just didn't realize they were love."

"You love me?" Grinning, he claimed her lips for a kiss. "And I love you." Another kiss. Becca clung to him as if he was everything to her, and something inside him opened.

But before he could put words to that, what sounded like a throat being cleared broke the silence. They turned to see Odette staring at them, a snake wrapped around one arm.

"I see my work here is done. The gods have spoken."

Zachary wondered for a moment if the voodoo priestess meant them or the murderer.

Odette turned her attention to Janet Phillippe's

daughter. She hovered over the prisoner and mumbled something. Danielle twitched, but her eyes didn't lose that vacant look. And then Odette turned her back on her.

"I will tell my people to go home," she said as regally as any queen. "Our work here tonight is done. You know where to find me."

Zachary watched her go and, pulling Becca tightly to his side, called the station.

Though an ambulance arrived quickly, the paramedics couldn't seem to bring Danielle out of her waking sleep....

SEEING JORDAN walk out of a jail cell and back into the squad room where he belonged was one of the best moments in Zachary's life. Nearly everyone but Gary Yancy was there to applaud his release. First Jordan kissed Camille DuPree until he got a standing ovation. Then he pumped Simone Jones's hand in thanks, after which he hugged and slapped Liam on the back and did the same to Zachary.

"Zach, I understand you're the man," Jordan said, grinning at him and pulling Camille close to his side.

Chest tight with emotion, Zachary tried to deny it. "Everyone was working together on your behalf."

"But you're the one who cracked the case and got Jordan off the hook," Liam insisted to his surprise.

Simone stood at Liam's side nodding in agreement, her hand around his arm. "You and Rebecca Romero."

Although she was hanging back, Becca was beaming at him, Zachary realized.

They hadn't had a moment alone since the night before. There'd been a flurry of activity on arriving at the station. The DMV report had confirmed that Lisa Cantro

really was Danielle Ambrose. Her confession to them
out in the bayou was backed up by the evidence they
found in her apartment—gris-gris, photographs, a diary.
Enough to free Jordan. They'd been up all night making
sure of it.

"Romero's going to need a new partner," Jordan
said, staring at Zach. "After what Yancy pulled, he'll
be lucky if he's not put behind bars."

If only they could prove Yancy had planted that poison, Zachary thought. Then realizing his brother's implication, he started. "Me? But I'm not a detective."

"You will be if I have anything to say about it,"
Becca told him, "because I'm recommending you."

"And I'll second that," Liam said. "In the mean-
time, I have an invitation for you. Our parents' thirtieth
anniversary party. We've been planning it for months."

"I…I don't know."

"Both Mom and Dad want you there," Jordan said.
Liam added. "So do we. It's time we recognized
everyone in the family."

Swallowing the lump in his throat, Zachary nodded.
"Then I would be honored."

"They need you as part of the family," Becca said,
pulling him to one side. "And we need more men like
you in the detective division."

"But what do *you* need?" he asked.

"I need you. I always have. You're a great cop and
an even better human being, *human* being the key word.
So we have different styles. We both want the same
thing."

"I hope so," he murmured. "Even if we don't get
to be partners in crime, *chère,* we could choose to be
partners in life."

"Is that a proposal, or are you simply trying to charm me?"

He shrugged and grinned at her. "What do you think?"

Melting into his arms, Becca murmured, "Convince me."

HARLEQUIN®
INTRIGUE®

has a new lineup of books to keep you on
the edge of your seat throughout the winter.
So be on the alert for...

Bold and brash—these men have sworn to serve
and protect as officers of the law...and only the
most special women can "catch" these good guys!

UNDER HIS PROTECTION
BY AMY J. FETZER
(October 2003)

UNMARKED MAN
BY DARLENE SCALERA
(November 2003)

BOYS IN BLUE
A special 3-in-1 volume with
REBECCA YORK (Ruth Glick writing as Rebecca York),
ANN VOSS PETERSON AND PATRICIA ROSEMOOR
(December 2003)

CONCEALED WEAPON
BY SUSAN PETERSON
(January 2004)

GUARDIAN OF HER HEART
BY LINDA O. JOHNSTON
(February 2004)

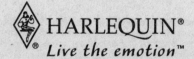

HARLEQUIN®
Live the emotion™

Visit us at www.eHarlequin.com
and www.tryintrigue.com

HIBBONTS

If you enjoyed what you just read,
then we've got an offer you can't resist!

Take 2 bestselling
love stories FREE!

Plus get a FREE surprise gift!

Clip this page and mail it to Harlequin Reader Service

IN U.S.A.
3010 Walden Ave.
P.O. Box 1867
Buffalo, N.Y. 14240-1867

IN CANADA
P.O. Box 609
Fort Erie, Ontario
L2A 5X3

YES! Please send me 2 free Harlequin Intrigue® novels and my free surprise gift. After receiving them, if I don't wish to receive anymore, I can return the shipping statement marked cancel. If I don't cancel, I will receive 6 brand-new novels each month, before they're available in stores! In the U.S.A., bill me at the bargain price of $3.99 plus 25¢ shipping and handling per book and applicable sales tax, if any*. In Canada, bill me at the bargain price of $4.74 plus 25¢ shipping and handling per book and applicable taxes**. That's the complete price and a savings of at least 10% off the cover prices—what a great deal! I understand that accepting the 2 free books and gift places me under no obligation ever to buy any books. I can always return a shipment and cancel at any time. Even if I never buy another book from Harlequin, the 2 free books and gift are mine to keep forever.

182 HDN DU9K
382 HDN DU9L

Name _____ (PLEASE PRINT) _____

Address _____ Apt.# _____

City _____ State/Prov. _____ Zip/Postal Code _____

* Terms and prices subject to change without notice. Sales tax applicable in N.Y.
** Canadian residents will be charged applicable provincial taxes and GST.
  All orders subject to approval. Offer limited to one per household and not valid to
  current Harlequin Intrigue® subscribers.
® are registered trademarks of Harlequin Enterprises Limited.

INT03

eHARLEQUIN.com

For **FREE online reading,** visit
www.eHarlequin.com now and enjoy:

Online Reads
Read **Daily** and **Weekly** chapters from
our Internet-exclusive stories by your
favorite authors.

Red-Hot Reads
Turn up the heat with one of our more
sensual online stories!

Interactive Novels
Cast your vote to help decide how these
stories unfold...then stay tuned!

Quick Reads
For shorter romantic reads, try our
collection of Poems, Toasts, & More!

Online Read Library
Miss one of our online reads?
Come here to catch up!

Reading Groups
Discuss, share and rave with other
community members!

For great reading online,
visit www.eHarlequin.com today!

HARLEQUIN®
INTRIGUE®

Our unique brand of high-caliber romantic suspense just cannot be contained. And to meet our readers' demands, Harlequin Intrigue is expanding its publishing lineup to include **SIX** breathtaking titles every month!

Here's what we have in store for you:

❏ A trilogy of **Heartskeep** stories by Dani Sinclair

❏ More great **Bachelors at Large** books featuring sexy, single cops

❏ Plus outstanding contributions from your favorite Harlequin Intrigue authors, such as Amanda Stevens, B.J. Daniels and Gayle Wilson

MORE variety.
MORE pulse-pounding excitement.
MORE of your favorite authors and series.
Every month.

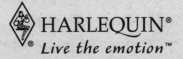

HARLEQUIN®
® *Live the emotion*™

Visit us at www.tryIntrigue.com

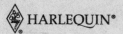

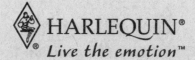